THE RULE OF WON

Also by Stefan Petrucha

Teen, Inc.

THE RULE OF WON

STEFAN PETRUCHA

Walker & Company
New York

First published in the United States of America in 2008 by Walker Publishing Company, Inc.
Visit Walker & Company's Web site at www.walkeryoungreaders.com

For information about permission to reproduce selections from this book, write to Permissions, Walker & Company, 175 Fifth Avenue, New York, New York 10010

Library of Congress Cataloging-in-Publication Data
Petrucha, Stefan.
The Rule of Won / Stefan Petrucha. — 1st ed.
p. cm.
Summary: Caleb Dunne, the quintessential slacker, is pressured by his girlfriend to join a high school club based on The Rule of Won, which promises to fulfill members' every "crave," but when nonbelievers start being ostracized and even hurt, Caleb must act.
ISBN-13: 978-0-8027-9651-6 • ISBN-10: 0-8027-9651-6
[1. Success—Fiction. 2. Supernatural—Fiction. 3. Clubs—Fiction. 4. Cliques (Sociology)—Fiction. 5. High school—Fiction. 6. Schools—Fiction. 7. Books and reading—Fiction.] I. Title.
PZ7.P44727Rul 2008 [Fic]—dc22 2008000255

Book design by Donna Mark
Typeset by Westchester Book Composition
Printed in the U.S.A. by Quebecor World Fairfield
2 4 6 8 10 9 7 5 3 1

All papers used by Walker & Company are natural, recyclable products made from wood grown in well-managed forests. The manufacturing processes conform to the environmental regulations of the country of origin.

Dedicated fondly to all of us who, despite the evidence, still expect the world to be exactly like what we picture in our heads . . .

"Some of my cousins who had the great advantage of University education used to tease me with arguments to prove that nothing has any existence except what we think of it. The whole creation is but a dream; all phenomena are imaginary. You create your own universe as you go along. The stronger your imagination, the more variegated your universe. When you leave off dreaming, the universe ceases to exist. These amusing mental acrobatics are all right to play with. They are perfectly harmless and perfectly useless. I warn my younger readers only to treat them as a game."

—Winston Churchill

THE RULE OF WON

Prologue

"Garish."

It was a word Alyssa Skinson had liked ever since she'd first heard it. It was what some old woman called the flowers at Alyssa's mother's funeral.

"Garish"—something that wanted to be lovely but was trying way too hard.

Like Alyssa, right now. Tightly wrapped in the old pink and green leggings Mom had knitted for her when she was nine, her legs pointed out over the roof edge. They were straight and lean and brightly colored. Her old yellow dress shoes sparkled on her feet like flames, making the leggings look like two burning birthday candles.

So . . . why not make a wish?

She looked around.

At her old house (silly to say because it was newer than this place) the night sky always held secret patches of color: blues, purples, greens. She'd even seen a moon-bow once, a night rainbow, so dim it didn't reflect in the pool. Here, though, the Screech Neck haze made everything gray. Even the stars looked sickly.

Why not wish for color?

She scrunched her face, forming an image in her head. When nothing happened, she tried harder. She tried so hard, she pressed her legs against the swollen gutters, making a stream of brown rainwater roll along her calves, darkening the leggings. Thick drops gathered on the heels of her yellow shoes and tumbled to the dry grass below.

"What're you doing?"

A shadow stood inside the dormer, gray as the town of Screech Neck, the ceiling light behind it as sickly as this poor little city's stars. She tried to ignore the shadow, but it leaned out of the darkness and became flesh and blood, pointy nose and square shoulders, curly hair and hazel eyes that looked like Mom's.

"What do you think you're doing out there, Alyssa?" Ethan asked.

She wanted to answer, but talking to her older brother was hard lately. He'd changed. He didn't even put on his sneakers the same way. He used to slip his feet in and out with the laces still tied. Now he carefully untied and tied them, like he was afraid of ruining them.

"You'll catch pneumonia."

He used to work an hour a day training at his martial arts, showing off his high kicks and fast punches. Now that they couldn't afford classes, he hadn't even unpacked his trophies.

"Dad'll have a fit."

He wasn't as smart as he used to be either. He used to read two or three books at a time, not just the same one over and over and over. It was like the move here had dulled him the same way it had dulled the sky.

"I'm looking for the aurora borealis," she said.

"Ha. It's like a million miles north. You have to be in Alaska. Or England."

"Stars are farther, and you can see them."

"The angle's wrong."

"If I keep wishing, it could happen."

That, he didn't challenge. He didn't dare, because of that book. Instead, he quietly poked his head farther out and they both stared at the sky awhile.

Was it really since the move that he'd changed? Or since he'd read *The Rule of Won*?

"It really can't happen, you know," Alyssa finally said, annoyed to have to contradict her own game. "You believe that book too much. It's just words."

He smiled like he knew it all. "They're the only words that can explain what *you* do."

"It's just a game. It's not like I've done anything impossible, like make something fly," she said with a sigh.

"I bet you could. I bet you could make something fly. You could probably even get Dad his old job back if you didn't like homeschooling so much."

Her face turned red. "That's not fair! I could not!" she cried. "And besides, I miss the academy, too, Ethan, but I think Dad's happier now."

"At half the salary? Losing our house? Look where we wound up. You think he likes Screech Neck? Do you think *anyone* does?"

"After Mom died, he thought it was more important for him to be around us. It was a good decision. And I couldn't change any of it even if I wanted to."

He pursed his lips. "You got the electricity to come on."

That again.

When they had first moved into this small "fixer-upper," they had had candles for light and bags of ice in coolers for the milk, eggs, and butter. The power company had said it'd be weeks before they could get someone out to fix the line. Technically they weren't even allowed to be living there, but Dad thought it'd be like camping. It wasn't. When the sun set, each room stacked with unpacked boxes, it was more like being buried in a cardboard tomb.

So, just to make herself feel better, Alyssa drew a picture of her new home the way she wanted it to be, all neat and brightly lit. A few hours after she finished, the lights flickered on and the refrigerator hummed. It seemed the house had come to life just because she'd wanted it to.

Which is what Ethan thought had happened.

She kind of liked the idea when she thought he was playing, but that was before she realized how serious he was, how so much of what he believed was right out of that book.

"You're so stupid, Ethan. The power company just fixed it early."

He ignored the insult. "What about Sam, your lost stuffed bear? You drew a picture of that, too, didn't you?"

Her eyes narrowed. She'd hidden that picture. "You went through my things."

"Well?"

"I talked to Aunt Sarah about it on the phone after I drew the picture. It made her look for it again in Mom's stuff, and she found it and sent it to me."

"Liar. You didn't call her."

"I did. I swear!"

Ignoring her vow, Ethan pulled himself inside, turning back into a shadow.

"You'll still draw the pictures I ask for?"

She rolled her eyes. "Yes."

He grunted and vanished, probably to his room to work on his notes for the big after-school meeting tomorrow with all the other people who read *The Rule of Won* over and over and over.

She didn't mind helping him, even if it was stupid. Maybe if she helped him, he'd go back to being a little more like the way he was. Not so angry. Not so . . . garish.

Alyssa sat there a while, in her wet leg warmers, trying as hard as she could to see some color in the gray. But her legs were cold, there was grit in the fabric, and the memory of her brother's voice buzzed like a bee in her head.

The spell broken, she sighed and went inside.

As a proud self-avowed slacker, I've actually been accused of being un-American, but the fact is I just don't want anything badly enough to have to work for it. Stuff? Nope, got some. Riches? Thanks but no thanks. Power? Not unless I can fly. Love? Well, you never really *own* love, do you?

To my mind this attitude, despite popular belief, is not an indication of laziness but evidence of a higher state of being. I feel I've achieved a near-perfect state. Here I am, Caleb Dunne, scruffy hair, brown eyes, lousy dresser, just sixteen—at peace with practically everything.

It turns out, though, there's a problem with this way of being. When you don't want anything yourself, all sorts of people pop out of the woodwork to want things for you. Spiritually speaking, this can be a pain. In my case, ever since an ugly incident last January, the following flies were in my buttermilk and would not shoo:

Mom wanted me to get a job.

Grandpa Joey wanted me to get a good swift kick in the ass.

My math teacher, Mr. Eldridge, wanted me to start thinking seriously about college.

Mrs. Ditellano, my creative writing teacher, wanted me to "float" along the river of my "deep self" to discover my "true purpose." That might be kind of pleasant if it didn't sound so much like drowning.

Even Dr. Wyatt, principal of Screech Neck High, was in on it. He wasn't so interested in me finding my true purpose in life, though, and instead wanted me . . .

"off the streets"

"away from decent folk"

before I did some

"real damage."

(I think that's sort of like a poem, which may be like floating, but I'm not sure. I'll have to ask Mrs. D.)

Last but in no way least, of course, was my go-getting girlfriend, the slight, hyperenergetic Vicky Bainbridge, who wanted me to have "grounding." Vicky B is the opposite of a slacker, always working on something: selling handmade cards in elementary school, volunteering at an ad agency in middle school, now running for public office (student body president) in high school. The yin to my yang, she completed me the way others might complete a midterm algebra exam (more on that later).

The morning Vicky spelled out her expectations for me, we stood in a poorly lit hallway of Screech Neck High School, just before classes began. She had a "Vote Vicky" button pinned on the chest of a tight green shirt. Beneath the bold words was a color photo of her pretty, perky face. Both the real Vicky and her button smiled with equal enthusiasm.

Only one of them spoke.

"*The Rule of Won,* Caleb. It'll change your life if you work at it. And, let's face it, you need grounding—badly," Vicky said. "So you'll go?"

It wasn't a question really, more a demand. She rapped her long nails, painted with tiger stripes, against the tile wall, waiting for me to say yes.

I, of course, wanted to say no, especially since she'd used the "w" word, "work." I wanted to explain how, historically, mankind's work ethic is pretty new, and IMHO, has yet to prove itself. I prefer the ancient Greeks, who thought it better to laze around philosophizing while some other poor slobs built the temples and farmed the crops. They believed the *more* leisure time you had to contemplate life, the better a person you became. And I was out to be the best person I could possibly be.

But here she was with her big grin, her straw-blond hair, and her shapely green shirt, insisting otherwise.

It wasn't always this way. Once, for better or worse, I was left to my own devices. That is, before that fateful day last January.

It was a snowy afternoon during winter break, and with Mom working overtime at the mall, as usual, and GP Joey taking up the couch in our small apartment, as usual, things at home were painfully boring. So I was out braving the cold, doing what I do best, wandering aimlessly, when I reached the grounds of Screech Neck High.

SNH, built in 1935 and looking every bit its age, is shaped like a broken T. About a decade ago, it was a total T, but the wing containing the gym and a couple of classrooms collapsed during a major storm. Just last year they finally, finally found the money to fix it.

Having jack else to do, I slipped through the chain-link fence surrounding the construction area to check it out. Frozen dirt crunched underfoot as I climbed a small hill for a good view. I was thinking it was pretty cool. The big sheets of plastic covering the tall windows flapped in the cold wind, letting out little wisps of that new gym smell.

But then the wacky Fates decided to mess with me. With an ungodly loud creak, like the rusty hinges on a giant-size door opening, the roof and the whole side wall collapsed, bringing down scaffolding and bricks and cinder blocks and wood and letting loose a major cloud of crap that billowed and rushed toward me. Before I could even think of moving, I was covered in junk and coughing concrete dust.

I was still coughing when I heard the sirens. The crash had tripped some alarm, and the police were on their way. There was yours truly, trespassing, covered in dust. I felt like a kid about to be caught with his hand in the cookie jar, only I didn't even get a cookie.

Knowing Screech Neck's finest wouldn't believe some sixteen-year-old slacker punk even if I swore I hadn't touched a thing, I booked, leaving a lovely trail of concrete dust footprints on the sidewalk. That much would have been fine since the prints vanished after a block and I could run pretty quickly.

The kicker was that my fellow classmate, super-nerd and wannabe ace reporter All-den Moore, was also out and about that day, doing whatever it is wannabe ace reporters do on snowy afternoons. His name's just plain Alden, but I make the the first syllable long—All-den. Kind of a holdover from elementary school when everyone used to make fun of him. Anyway, after the collapse, he saw me running, covered in dust. Mind like a steel trap, he put two and two together and got five.

Did he tell? Of course.

I was in the shower scraping wet gunk off my skin when the cops came to the door. GP Joey, the world's only honest auto mechanic (part of the reason his business was failing) handed over my dust-caked clothes and explained how it wasn't my fault I was turning out badly, since my deadbeat dad ran off when I was three, and with him and Mom working all the time, there was no one around to give me proper supervision.

Lucky for me, they still couldn't quite press charges. What with there being no actual vandalism, there was no actual evidence of vandalism.

Unlucky for me, Principal Wyatt didn't care about evidence. Unlike the courts, his rule of thumb was—if he feels like it's true, it's true. He felt like I was guilty and suspended me for the rest of the school year. I think the worst part was the look on my mother's face when she found out.

As a final capper to the worst winter I'd had since I found out there was no Santa Claus (*No jolly guy who just brings you stuff? Say it ain't so, Ma!*), it turned out the construction company didn't have the proper insurance, so SNH not only remained a broken T, but everyone, from the students to the teachers to the custodial staff, blamed me.

I suppose I should've just been grateful Vicky stuck by me when I returned that September. Even if we hadn't been alone once since then. Even if, as she explained that morning, there were . . . conditions.

"Caleb, no one talks to you anymore. You've got to pull yourself out of this," Vicky said. "The meeting will help. I promise. They'll accept you."

Silence hung in the air like a smelly old sock on a doorknob. "I haven't even read the book," I said lamely.

"It's an Open Crave."

I raised an eyebrow. "A what?"

I could tell she was trying to be patient. "*The Rule of Won* is about fulfilling desires, so they call the meetings 'Craves.' Open Craves are for people just starting out."

"Like Open Graves are for people just finishing up?"

I thought that was worth a chuckle. She didn't.

"This isn't middle school anymore. I'm trying to make something of myself. I don't want to have to leave you behind."

"Vicky, you've been trying to make something of yourself since you were two. And really, you're running for student council, not Congress. It's no big deal."

Her eyes narrowed with anger. "No. It's what I make of it. Promise you'll go."

"I don't know, Vick . . ."

She pulled her trump card. "My parents don't even want me talking to you. They're convinced you're a no-account vandal who needs to be in jail."

I felt defeated, but I pretended I still had my pride. "They're wrong, but so what? So what if I don't care about college? So what if I don't want to bust my ass getting some corporate lackey job so I can make a lot of money? I mean, what's the big deal?"

"The big deal, Caleb, is that sometimes you have to move forward just to avoid going backward. Wyatt's looking for an excuse to get rid of you. So's most of the school. So are my parents. Maybe . . . so am I."

I sighed. "Fine. I'll go."

She smiled, like her button. I didn't, like me, and we split to enjoy our day, me with a sinking feeling in my gut, hoping this Crave thing wouldn't entail homework.

Truth be told, slacker though I was, there was something I did want for myself: to turn back the clock to last year when I had a decent average without having to study, a girlfriend who didn't mind my lack of ambition—and no arrest record.

But it didn't look like that was going to happen any time soon.

First period was creative writing, but I was in no hurry to get there. I try not to be in a hurry to get anywhere. I ambled nice and slow, but people kept staring at me, since I was apparently guilty until proven innocent. One girl even hissed. After that, I picked up my pace.

I was a little relieved to see Erica Black, the only other

person in the school who spoke to me, sitting on the floor near the classroom door. She was willing to talk to me, I think, because she had transferred in this year and didn't know my sordid past. Frankly, she made me nervous. She's a little dark and intense, which explained why no one bothered to mention to her that I was the maniac who blew up the school.

She was hunched over, scribbling in a spiral-bound notebook. No shock there. She was *always* writing—on the bus, at lunch, in the halls. Writing, writing, writing. Hell, I don't do things I *like* that often.

At least she was company, so I walked over.

"What's up, Erica?"

"Just contemplating the darkness that is my soul," she said.

That's how she talks.

"Cool," I shot back, being what they call "ironic."

I squinted at the page, expecting a poem about how much better darkness is than light, but it was all numbers.

"Not polite to stare, Mr. Dunne," she said.

Don't get me wrong, Erica Black was cute as hell. At first glance, you might think she's Goth (SNH has three), but she's not. She does have that Goth look. Wan. Glum. She also has this black curly hair, and I mean *black* like a night sky, but it's short, and she keeps most of it covered with this old-style 1920s hat that looks like a lacy baseball cap. Her skin is smooth without a freckle or a drop of acne. It always shines a little, too, like a dinner plate.

I looked at the top of her hat and stated the obvious: "That's not a poem."

She answered, either annoyed or pretending to be: "No. It's not. Did you want a poem? Fine. Here:

Razors pain you; Rivers are damp;
Acids stain you; And drugs cause cramp.
Guns aren't lawful; Nooses give;
Gas smells awful; You might as well live.

"Dorothy Parker, 1926."

"Wow. Parker, eh? I thought it was yours for sure."

"Really? You thought I wrote a poem about suicidal depression? That's the sweetest thing anyone's ever said to me!" She flashed this big fake smile that almost seemed to be making fun of Vicky's button. "But the fact is, if I don't pass my next algebra test, I *will* kill myself."

I rolled my eyes.

"Get off it. Pigeons and gerbils can pass Blubaugh's tests. They're all multiple choice and she lets you retake them. Believe me, I know. I scored the lowest in the class the first time, but I passed. You'd have to be brain-dead."

She eyed me. "Then disconnect me from life support, because I failed three. As a reward, my parents had me moved into Mr. *Eldridge's* class."

I gasped. "Ow. That's like teaching someone to swim by tying lead weights to their feet."

She nodded. "Yeah. Better teacher, tougher tests. The only math tests in the world with essay questions. It's bringing down my whole average and ruining any chance I have of getting a scholarship."

The bell rang. She clapped the book shut and stood. "On the other hand, I hear getting really drunk and freezing to death can actually be pleasant, like falling asleep."

"You'd never do that," I told her.

"Why not?"

"Because then you'd miss your own funeral."

I caught a real smile on her face as she went inside. "Good point."

Some people might be worried about the way she was talking about suicide, but really, it was her way of blowing off steam. Frankly, I didn't know anyone who had Eldridge that didn't contemplate offing themselves at some point. I had him for trig this year, and even though I was doing fine without much effort, I was having regular night terrors about the quadratic equation slipping into my bedroom and eating my brain.

Vicky had already left me feeling pretty glum, but my mood dropped further when I walked into creative writing and saw an assignment on the board to write three "free-verse" poems, each about a different feeling. Mrs. Ditellano smiled at me. She has a friendly, plump face and wears these square glasses, like Mrs. Santa Claus, only creepy.

"Are we floating today, Caleb?"

I looked at my feet. "Don't seem to be, Mrs. D."

"Keep working at it, dear. You'll get there."

Honestly? I only signed up for creative writing because I

wanted to write science fiction, with particle beams and warp engines and alien tentacles that reach through your nose into your respiratory system and lay eggs that burst your lungs. Instead, it turned out to be all this "floating."

I scribbled some nonsense about air and waves and my soul, then spent the rest of the class worrying about the Crave. As the day wore on I took a break from fretting to consider talking to All-den Moore. I hadn't spoken to him since I'd gotten back, and rumor had it he was afraid I was going to beat the crap out of him. He's a nervous kid to begin with. Since I didn't really blame him for turning me in—he was just being honest, after all—I wanted him to know things were okay, but I didn't see him in the halls or at lunch.

I did see Dr. Wyatt. He's a little guy in a suit, kind of like Quark from *Star Trek: Deep Space Nine,* but without the personality. When he saw me, he pointed at me and practically shouted, "I'm watching you, Dunne!"

Maybe, but he wasn't watching the door opening in front of him, and *wham*! He slammed right into it, nose first.

I hightailed it out of there, figuring he'd blame that on me, too.

After all, I was responsible for accidents, right?

Most things are easier said than done, but for a slacker, that's true of *everything*. Picture your normal nervousness going to a club the first time, with people you mostly don't know, who probably hate you, to discuss a book you haven't read that you'd probably hate if you did. Triple it—that's how I felt about that first Crave.

Even before the building collapse I wasn't a public kind of guy. Plus, for someone who prided himself on wanting *nothing*, a meeting about getting what you wanted was a trip into the lion's den. Creative writing, with the floating, was bad enough.

Most of all, though, I dreaded the possibility of a group hug. You get into a circle with a lot of people like that and you never really know who you're hugging, or who's hugging you. Ach.

So, even though I usually leaped giddily from my seat at the end of the day, instead I slogged along like a slug. Eventually exiting from SNH's rear end, I entered a truly ugly asphalt plain. Once a parking lot, it was now home to a series of rickety trailers euphemistically called "temporary" classrooms. Just to see them brings to mind what GP Joey calls Screech Neck's unofficial town motto: Doing the worst with what little we have.

They were plopped down by some government relief agency after the school wing collapsed. They've been here longer than I have, and will probably still be here after I've gone. So, as far as SNH is concerned, I'm more temporary than they are.

It's in the trailers that most after-school clubs meet, except for the *Weekly Screech*, the school paper that comes out maybe once a year, if at all. They have an actual office with lots of room. I heard All-den was the new editor, lucky guy. As for the rest of us, Dr. Wyatt figures if we trash these old wrecks, no one will notice or care.

I approached trailer B, thudded up the three metal steps, sighed for my forgotten dignity, and went in. Before I even saw anything, I was blasted with the thick smell of mold so ancient it'd probably developed intelligence and was planning to start its own club.

Adding to that smell were ten, maybe fifteen kids. Huge crowd for one of our clubs. When they saw me, everyone inhaled. It was like one of those Westerns where the bad guy walks into the saloon.

I figured that was my cue to bag this scene, but Vicky and her button were sitting in a corner, both smiling in a come-hither way, so I gritted my teeth, pulled up a chair, and sat next to her. Sensing my distress, she gently scratched the back of my neck with those long painted fingernails of hers, making my brain melt. I closed my eyes, almost forgetting where I was until I opened them again and saw everyone ogling at me.

"Hey, I'm not selling tickets," I said.

Erica Black was there, too—the only one not focused on me. I didn't notice her at first because she was behind this huge Goth guy complete with black lipstick and vampire contact lenses. I tried waving, but she was too busy writing in her journal. Vicky, who never pays attention to me when I want her to, noticed me trying to wave to a cute girl. Instead of the gentle stroking, she grabbed a tuft of brown hair at the back of my head and yanked.

"Ow!"

Before I could explain we were just friends, a voice boomed through the trailer. It was deep but calm, suave, and authoritative, like James Bond just before he shoots you or Darth Vader asking you to join his plan to overthrow the empire and rule the universe together as father and son.

"Welcome to our first Crave," it said.

Still holding the back of my head, I looked up at the source of the voice—this guy who was what I'd call a little "too." He stood just a little too straight. His clothes, though just a T-shirt and jeans, were a little too clean. His shoelaces were a little too bright, like he bleached and ironed them every night. Even his demeanor was a little too self-assured, like he was a teacher, only he was a kid, like us.

Or, like us if we'd been born on Krypton.

It was Ethan Skinson, the kid who had called the meeting.

I had heard (well, really *over*heard, since no one talks to me) that he and his sister used to attend private school before their lawyer dad lost his high-paying job, their adjustable mortgage rate shot up, and their big-ass house went into foreclosure. Now they're Duppies (downwardly mobile), slumming in Screech Neck. This isn't to say Screech Neck is the poorest place in the world but, well, we're all a bit impressed when people show up with new loose-leaf paper.

He held a thick book, which he raised with both hands. With a flourish, he set it down on the cracked surface of a folding desk-chair, so the title, set in large type against a background showing an open hand and some ancient writing, faced us. There was also a glowing symbol on the cover, a "1" inside a diamond.

"We're here to put into practice the ideas in this book, *The Rule of Won* by Jasper Trelawney. To put it simply, the book explains that if you can completely *imagine* you've already achieved some goal in your life, you *will* win it."

I can barely say two words in front of a group without swallowing my tongue, but he was chugging along.

"Think about that," he said. "Anything you want. Money, fame, friends. The universe has *everything* in it and enough of everything for everybody. Like the book says, the difference between where you are and where you want to be is inside you."

"Right," I was thinking. "If the universe is really just a huge Wal-Mart and you've got unlimited credit, why doesn't everyone *already* have whatever they want?"

I didn't expect him to hear me, since I was thinking and not talking, but he said, "You're probably wondering: If it's that simple, then why doesn't everyone already have whatever they want?"

Now I added "a little too freaky" to the list.

"It's because we hold ourselves back, set up our own failures. Because of bad experiences, bad teaching, or just bad expectations, most of us expect the worst from life, so that's what most of us get. The universe *only* gives you what you ask for, so if you think about getting sick long enough, you'll get sick. If you imagine someone beating you up often enough, someone will beat you up. *But* . . . imagine getting a new car long enough and that'll happen, too. Imagine losing weight or gaining muscle, and you will."

Yeah? Funny, but I didn't remember asking for the freaking school to cave in, or for All-den to be there to rat me out, or for everyone to hate me. I didn't *want* any of that.

"Our every single thought does not become instantly real. It takes time and effort. Plant the thought, tend the thought, and the event will grow. Our thoughts are either our servants or our masters."

Ethan picked up the book and shook it at us, like the words in it were water and he could shower us with them. "You don't have to wonder or guess about any of this. We're going to prove it all here, ourselves, by using our *mesmories* to *imanifest* our *craves*."

Even if I didn't believe him, I was at least half following him until he started speaking in gibberish. Now I was like, "Do the who with what to where?"

"Let me give you an example."

Please.

"On the back of the door to my room there's a framed print of the *Proverbs of Hell* by William Blake. He's this eighteenth-century poet I couldn't care less about, but my mother left it to me when she died. When I wake up, it's the first thing I see; the last when I fall asleep. I see it so often that wherever I am I can close my eyes and picture it just as clearly as if it were in front of me."

He closed his eyes.

"Right now I can see the tear in the corner, a splinter sticking out the side of the frame, even the exact shape of a little apple juice stain above the 'P' in 'Proverbs.' This is called a 'mesmory,' a sense memory, something you can remember just as clearly as you can see. When you can picture your heart's desire as clearly as I can that poster, it's sure to be yours. Got it?"

Got it. Maybe.

He wrote quickly on the blackboard in neat block letters. "I've set up a private message board. Sign in with this password, real names only, and please don't share it with anyone outside the Crave. I want everyone who's interested to post Craves—things you want, but true things, maybe even things you think aren't even possible. Anything, really. Sky's the limit. Next meeting, I'll pick one out and we'll work on it together."

He turned back and gave us a smile like the one on Vicky's button. "I don't expect you to post your deepest secret desires. We don't know each other that well. But if you want results, take it seriously, and keep it real. Questions?"

I had a dozen, starting with, "How old are you, really—forty?"

But nobody else said anything so I kept my mouth shut. I did notice Vicky was looking at him with this funky sort of hungry expression.

"Wednesday we'll meet again and start imanifesting. Until then, thanks for coming!"

That was it. We stood up like it was the end of a class and moved for the door. No one hung back to talk to Ethan. Like I said, he had this "teacher" vibe, and no one hung back to talk to teachers unless they were failing.

Knowing how the whole not-being-talked-to thing felt, I gave him a nod. My nods are quick, jerky things. You have to be watching to catch them. He caught it and nodded back, this little smile frozen on his face as he smoothly moved his chin up and down. It was, like, a little too-perfect nod.

I didn't know whether I wanted to be his friend or drive a stake through his heart.

Thankfully, no one bothered glaring at me as we left. I guess they were all thinking about Ethan. Vicky kept looking over her shoulder at him, like he was a UFO, so I turned back once or twice myself. I couldn't tell if he was disappointed or excited with how the meeting had gone. Just like I didn't know if going to this stupid meeting about this stupid book had helped me with Vicky or not.

As we walked, I tried to say hello to Erica again, but she was still too busy writing in her spiral-bound. I wondered if she took showers with that thing. This was an interesting thought, so I started imagining her taking showers, she and her journal all covered in suds.

Vicky, breaking my concentration, gave me a bubbly smile and said, "So? What'd you think of the meeting?"

I opted to grunt.

She shook her head, reached into her backpack, and pulled out a brightly gift-wrapped present.

"Here," she said.

"Wow," I said. "Thanks!"

I love presents. They're, like, not only free, they also mean someone likes you enough to give you something. I was pretty happy for a second there, until I realized what it was. The giveaway was a little bronze pin on top of the ribbon, diamond shaped with a "1" in the center—the symbol of *The Rule of Won*.

"Oh."

The symbol was also on the cover of the paperback inside the wrapping. Joy.

"You couldn't spring for the DVD?" I asked, half joking.

She leaned over and put the pin on the collar of my overshirt. It's an old green service station shirt, complete with some oil stains. Joey gave it to me. I usually wear it over a T-shirt. With the pin on it, it suddenly felt totally goofy.

"Vicky, I'm not sure about any of this."

Actually, I was pretty sure I didn't want anything to do with this Crave crap, but I didn't want to tell her that. "How about you give me a campaign button instead?"

Her lips curled. "Uh . . . not so sure that would help my campaign, you know? My opponent's already making a big deal about how you and I used to date."

"Used to? Wait a minute . . . did we stop?"

She pushed the book flat against my chest, like she'd get it inside me one way or another. "Read it," she said. "It's not long, and there are lots of pictures. Let it change you."

"Vicky . . ."

She poked a long nail into the "1" pin on my shirt. "And take your Crave seriously."

"Vicky—"

"Just for two weeks, okay? If it doesn't work, if it doesn't help you, then quit. Okay? But please? Two weeks? Next meeting is Wednesday."

"Fine," I said. Ignoring her whole "used to" comment, I asked, "Want to walk to Java Jive and grab some—"

She shook her head. "Sorry, Caleb. I've got lots of homework and a campaign speech to polish."

Before she turned, she flashed a big grin. "Maybe you should make being alone with me again your Crave!"

Yeah, right. Like I was going to post on a message board about how my girlfriend didn't want to go out with me. What wonders *that* would do for my self-esteem. And hell, after listening to Ethan, I was wondering if I *had* made the freaking gym fall down. Maybe because I was secretly feeling guilty about being a slacker. Right.

But, disbelief aside, I gotta confess, I kind of liked the basic idea. As a slacker, the notion that my life could change without me actually doing anything other than thinking about it *sounded* good.

At the bus stop I finally saw good old All-den Moore. He was bogged down with all these books and loose papers. I hadn't spotted him earlier because he'd changed. He used to be a heavyset kid who wore pants that were too short. Now he'd lost some weight and either shrunk or gotten clothes that fit. Still seemed the nervous sort, though—the kind who'd twitch if you raised your hand too fast, like you might hit him.

He was busy trying to shove some of those papers into the old khaki army backpack he used for books. The thing was so full, you could see the thread unraveling at the seams. The more stuff he shoved in, the more slipped out, but he wouldn't give up. With both hands busy, he tried to catch the falling papers under his foot. It was like this weird, awkward dance.

I scooped some of the papers off the ground and held them out to him.

As soon as he recognized me, he was like a squirrel, looking all around and wincing.

"Caleb Dunne. You want to kill me," he said.

He snatched the papers from me and hopped about a yard or so away before trying to stuff them into his pack.

"All-den, it's okay, really. I don't want you to die. Not prematurely anyway."

"Just suffer, right?"

Once he realized I wasn't coming any closer, I got him to stay still long enough to say what I had to.

"No, I just want you to know, you did what you thought was right and I don't blame you. I'm not the bullying sort. Too much effort. You don't have to be afraid."

He looked around again, then at me. "I'm not afraid of you. I'm only sorry they didn't throw you in juvie," he half muttered under his breath.

"But I didn't do anything!"

"Then why'd you run?"

"Unbelievable. Because I thought if someone saw me there, they might think I *had* done something. And I was right, wasn't I?"

He grunted. He still didn't believe me. I guess no one did. Maybe Vicky didn't either.

His bus pulled up. He backed up to the doors, keeping his eyes on me like I was going to steal his precious papers. Then he squinted at the button Vicky gave me and did a double take.

"*The Rule of Won?*"

"Yeah. What of it?"

He shrugged. "It's only the most incredibly inane book on the entire planet."

I wanted to say I was just wearing the damn thing for Vicky, but that'd sound pretty lame, too, eh?

"No, wait, I don't . . . I'm just . . ."

As I babbled, he got on the bus.

If that little encounter didn't make me feel all warm and cozy, as the bus pulled out, it farted a big black cloud of exhaust right in my face.

I guess Ethan would say that I'd asked for it.

- Ten million dollars would be terrific. I'll do the rest. Thanks. All best. —Dylan

- What I really want most of all right now is to earn the trust of our student body by being elected its president. I just know I could do the best job of anyone running, and I want to devote all my spare time to making our school a better place. So please vote for me! —Vicky

- I want the proportional strength of a spider. If granted this boon, I swear I will always remember that with great strength comes great responsibility. —Jacob

- The picture is simple and stark: Curly paper edges crammed with handwritten solutions to the Great Unknown X. Red check after red check. No blood, no error, only certainty. It's algebra, sweet algebra, oh hated friend and foe. I want to pass you, ace you, beat you, swallow you whole, so that even Mr. Eldridge, with his great unclean mustache, shall smile his smile upon me, and the sun will shine and I will get the scholarship that will enable me to go to Hampshire Arts College. Absolutely totally. —Erica

- OMG! I'm so thrilled we finally have a place to talk about this amazing book and its ideas! Thank you, Ethan! I've been a fan ever since its first edition and I can't wait to see the results I know we'll get. Do you guys know that Jasper Trelawney didn't exactly write the book himself? He'd self-published another book, *Sitting on the Secret Self*, that only sold, like, a hundred copies. I mean, the guy was in his thirties and living in his mother's garage. One day he got a copy of it back in the mail. He figured it was someone asking for a refund, but then he noticed all these notes written in the margins, *correcting* his ideas. It was from those notes that he wrote *The Rule of Won*, which has sold tens of millions of copies and changed millions of lives! So I guess what I'd like for myself most of all is to meet the person who *really* wrote *The Rule of Won*. They must be totally amazing, right? —Grace

- If we're all going to be working on this together, why not do something that helps all of us? The school budget was cut by, like, half a million dollars last year; the arts program is practically gone; and aside from the fact that we don't have a gym, there's no cash for new equipment for the sports teams. How about we all wish for money for the school? —Dana

- I'm not sure my religion allows me to believe in the fulfillment of all my desires until *after* I'm dead, so I think I have to quit your club. Sorry. —Luke

- I would like the greatest gaming system in the world, the Xbox. A 733 MHz Intel main processor and 233 MHz graphics processor from nVidia create photorealistic graphics in real time. A huge hard drive stores saved games and characters, and a built-in Ethernet port enables super-fast multiplayer online gaming over a broadband Internet connection. —Landon

- My parents are going away next weekend and I would absolutely love it if they decided to let me stay home alone, despite the ugly incident last time involving sixteen kids, some of whom I didn't even really know, and Mom's collection of porcelain figurines, which really wasn't my fault. —Jane

- A new iPod. I lost my old one, right out of my locker. I think someone knows the combination. —Sally

- There's someone I really care about who doesn't know I care about him, and I'd like him to know how I feel without having to tell him. We're sort of in different cliques, though. Do I have to mention a name? —Kathleen

- Sorry, my dog ate my craving. —Mike

- Okay, I'm taking this seriously. I want people to stop staring at me like they want to kill me. I want them to believe me when I say I had nothing to do with the gym collapsing. All this glaring makes me want to scream and make a scene, and if I do, I'll get expelled. So, a little help here? —Caleb

- I've always wanted exactly what I want whenever I want it, so this club seems great for me! There's this terrific tank top that would look killer on me if only it came in slate gray to match the highlights on my jeans. They have every color, pastels to neon, except a nice slate gray. I would love it if one of those showed up. —Beth

- I want to be able to do an ollie, like my brother, but I keep landing on my ass. You've got to roll forward and pop down hard on the tail with your back foot. When the nose starts to point up, you drag the front foot up, which causes the skateboard to drag up and get higher. You lift your back foot and eventually stop the drag while the skateboard stops rising. The back rises up to the same level as the other side of the skateboard. Then you land on all four wheels, rolling away. —Alex

- Nicole and I were BFF since grade school, but now that we're at Screech Neck High she's gone all tech-nerd on me and I can't understand a word she's saying. Last week she got this seriously tricked-out iPhone that makes everyone's eyes bug out. It's not that I'd like an iPhone like that myself, but I'd really like hers to break. —Sophia

You never know what you can do until you do it. Then again, you also never know what you shouldn't do until you do that. For instance, the moment I finished writing my Crave, even if I didn't believe in magic, I actually felt good about it. It was an honest, fearless expression of my feelings of alienation, a cry for help from my fellow man. Maybe it would even make people be nicer to me.

Seconds later, though, when it was posted on the board, I felt like a jerk. What was I thinking? Everyone who already hated me would laugh their asses off when they read it—Juvenile Delinquent Dunne doing the sensitive New Age guy thing.

Crap.

I even tried hiding my head under my overshirt as I made my way out of the Screech Neck Public Library, where I'd used the computer. Probably no one would have noticed if I'd just walked out, but because of the funny way I was moving, everyone stared.

Almost everyone. Ethan Skinson was at one of the terminals, straight-backed, shoelaces shining. It was surprising to see someone like him stuck at a public computer. I figured he'd have his own rig.

I didn't say hi because, well, I was trying to hide, but past that, I wasn't sure whether to call him Ethan or Mr. Skinson or My Crave Master. He was too busy to notice me anyway, probably reading my post and struggling to hold back the laughter.

As the days passed, though, the mockery I feared never materialized. Not everyone knew about the message board, I guess, and those who did had their own Craves to feel uncomfortable about. They rat me out, I rat them out. Mutually assured destruction. Like we all had nukes.

It did score me points with Vicky. She not only called it "brave," but by Wednesday, she had agreed to have a meal with me. Yeah, it was lunch, during school hours, and in the cafeteria, but it was a start. At least I thought it was a start.

After we'd loaded up our Styrofoam trays with steaming heaps of God-knows-what, instead of finding a quiet spot to chat, she led us right next to the table traditionally occupied by our b-ball team, the Screech Neck Basket Cases (I know . . . I didn't name them). They were hooting and carrying on as if they hadn't lost every single game they'd played. I guess you could chalk that up to the lack of a gym, but really, they just sucked. And they were loud. I could barely think, let alone talk.

"Get together after school?" I shouted at Vicky as one of

the players leaped up on the table and poured some soda on his screaming teammate.

"What?" she said, holding a hand to her ear. This week her fingernails had little rainbows on them. With her fingers all together against her head, they made a multicolored wavy line.

Annoyed, I tried to stab a soggy french fry with my spork. Damn spud was so springy, the tines kept bouncing off. Then the cheap spork snapped. Fed up, I grabbed a pen and paper from my notebook and wrote in nice block letters:

DO YOU WANT TO GO OUT TOGETHER AFTER SCHOOL?

I held it up for her to read.

"Oh," she said. "Not today, sorry! I'm hanging campaign posters!"

I scratched that out and wrote:

HOW ABOUT I HELP U?

"Uh . . . you don't have to do that! It's very, very sweet, but it's okay! I . . . I like to use it as an excuse to talk to people one-on-one!"

WOULDN'T WANT TO ROB U OF THAT JOY.

She gave me a look. "You don't have to write everything out!"

I'M IMANIFESTING.

She didn't laugh. She hadn't laughed at anything I'd said or done in a long time. Back in middle school, before we were dating, she used to break into hysterics whenever I so much as put a pencil halfway up my nose. Good times.

Frustrated, I tightened my hand on the pen and was about to jam it up my nostril when she grabbed my hand and mouthed, "Read the book."

I *really* didn't want to do that. It seemed like such a commitment for something I didn't believe in at all. Then again, I was still wearing that stupid "1" pin. I told myself I'd just forgotten to take it off my overshirt, which I wore every day, but I guess I was still hoping to impress her. I'd look at it every morning, sigh, and figure taking it off was more of an effort than leaving it on.

With the pin on, though, I noticed other kids wearing them, too—on shirts, backpacks, coats. One senior wore it in her pierced navel, which was certainly attention grabbing. Turns out there were more Crave People, or Cravers, or whatever they call themselves, at school than came to the meeting. It made me wonder if *The Rule* was really all that stupid.

Speaking of the meeting, at the end of the day, when I trotted out of the main building through a rainy afternoon and into that moldy stink-fest of a trailer, Mike, the jock who'd made a joke about his dog on the board, actually smiled and said, "Caleb, how's it going?"

A few of the others gave me "hello" nods when I sat.

Whoa. Maybe my Crave hadn't been so stupid.

Or maybe *The Rule of Won* sort of worked? Nah.

No one new showed. We even lost maybe five people, but those who remained seemed pretty into it. Erica was there again, writing away. I'd been so busy fretting about my post and trying to get Vicky to go out with me I hadn't realized until now that she hadn't been at creative writing all week. Probably skipped it to study algebra.

Vicky sat next to me and scratched gently at the back of my hair. Given how well lunch had gone, I shook my head, and she stopped. I do have some self-respect. Not a lot, but some.

Soon the dulcet tones of Ethan Skinson and his vocal stylings filled our ears. "Thanks for coming back."

He looked nervous this time. Not All-den nervous. More like he had too much energy. Every now and then his eyes would flash this wild mad scientist look. You'd think it would make him seem more human, but it didn't.

"I've brought something a little special that I'm pretty excited about, but before we get to that, I want to tell you how great it is that so many people posted Craves. Some weren't exactly serious, but like the book says, we have to understand things superficially before we understand them deeply. I guess making fun of something you don't understand is one way to get started on that."

You could tell he didn't mean that. Ethan obviously took this *very* seriously and didn't like it when someone else didn't. I turned back to Vicky, planning to whisper a joke about his shoelaces, when I noticed how serious *she* looked, and how her pupils dilated a bit as she watched him.

I knew she liked this guy. Now I was wondering how much. What with the way she'd treated me lately, it was starting to piss me off.

"Anyway, I've decided which Crave we should work on first . . ."

My hand shot up. "Mr. Skinson?"

Vicky stiffened. Everyone gave me a look. I was the first person other than Ethan to talk during a Crave. Whoop-dee-doo.

"Ethan," Ethan said, clueless I was joking with him.

"Mr. Ethan," I shot back. Mike and Erica stifled a chuckle. "I'm just, you know, wondering why you get to decide. Why don't we all vote on it?"

I felt Vicky shifting. I figured her hand was reaching for the back of my hair to yank it, but I leaned forward so she couldn't grab me without making it really obvious.

The question didn't bother Ethan. He seemed pleased someone had actually spoken to him.

"Fair enough, but when you vote, you have a 'winner' and a 'loser,' right?" he said. Yeah, he did that bizarre air-quote thing with his fingers. "If someone feels they've 'lost,' it makes it harder to give the 'winner' their full effort. Make sense?"

"Sort of," I said. But I was also remembering something Joey had said once—that the problem with democracy is that most people are idiots, but the problem with dictatorships is that *all* dictators are idiots.

"How about this?" Ethan said. "Anyone think it'd be a *bad* idea for Screech Neck High to get more funding?"

Dana, a lean girl with frizzy hair, the one who had written that Crave, beamed. It was a good move from Ethan. Who could object to that?

"Great," he said, clapping his hands and rubbing them. "Before we get down to actually imanifesting, I downloaded a meditation read by Jasper Trelawney and brought it along. I thought we could start by giving it a listen."

He half turned, and I noticed an iPod on a desk connected to a couple of speakers. Before he could press PLAY, Grace, the giddy Trelawney groupie, raised her hand and shook like she had to pee.

Apparently now that I'd broken the ice, it was okay for everyone to talk.

Even Ethan furrowed his brow at her a little. "Yes?"

She sang out, "Are you sure it's really him? There's a big rumor he hired a famous voice actor to play him. Some people say it's Russell Crowe, but I think it could be Ian McKellen."

"I don't know. But that's what it says on the download," Ethan answered.

"Oh," Grace said. "I thought maybe you knew more."

He shrugged good-naturedly. "Nope. Anyway, as far as I know, he wrote it, so relax, close your eyes if you want, sit back, and . . . listen."

Before anyone else could interrupt, he hit PLAY on the iPod, then sat down and closed his eyes. A high voice filled the room, nothing like Ian McKellen or Russell Crowe, or even Ethan. I glanced around the room and saw that most everyone had closed their eyes, even Erica. Mike hadn't yet. He eyed me with a shrug. I shrugged back and closed my eyes, too.

And the voice said:

I dream, sometimes, I've swum to the bottom of the ocean. I'm down so deep, have so many miles of water above me, there's no way I can ever swim back. It's a one-way trip. I knew that when I started. I've sacrificed my life to reach a door, a hole in the bottom of the world. Why? Because on the other side of the door lay the secrets of life, the universe, and everything.

Once it was easy to reach, as instinctive to embrace as breathing, but I've spent too many years away from it, too much time enslaved by petty distractions. It slipped away slowly at first, then faster, but now it's gone so far away the only thing left for it to do is vanish forever. The only chance I have to reach it again is by being willing to die for it.

Or maybe it's always been this far, and I've only imagined being closer. It doesn't matter. My lungs are about to pop like swollen balloons. I grit my teeth, wobble my diaphram up and down, trying to fool my body into thinking I'm giving it some air. My hands wrap around the iron rung in the door's center. They nearly slip off because of all the slime, but I hold on and pull myself down the final yard. I plant my heels on the sandy floor, brace my legs, brace my soul, and pull.

It's not enough. I'm not enough. The door's rusted shut. The rung threatens to break, rotted by time and ocean. I give it one last try.

A few last tiny bubbles roll from my lips up my face. Just as I'm about to give in to the suicidal longing of my body to inhale, the door gives, just an inch. In an instant, the sea floor is bathed in incredibly warm, soothing light, the light of God, of the universe, of the ultimate.

Then I wake up.

And everything I've dreamed is true.

It ended. Everyone looked up, but no one spoke. All you could hear for a while was the steady rain outside. The meditation, or whatever it was, made about as much sense to me as one of Mrs. D's poetry assignments, but I was feeling unusually calm, groggy even. I had to wonder if it was one of those secret subliminal hypnosis tapes, the kind that reprogrammed you without you even knowing.

Ethan spoke again. "I want everyone here right now to find themselves a mesmory. Pick the first one that comes to mind, anything—something in your room, a moment from a vacation, something cheerful if you can, but something that feels totally real."

I wasn't trying to make fun or anything, but the first thing that came to my mind, for whatever freaky reason, was that spork snapping against the french fry during lunch. It was a pretty solid memory—the plastic, the sound of the crunch, the roar of the cafeteria, that special oily french fry smell—so I went with it. I mean, why not? I was there, right?

"Got it? Hold on to that and chant with me, 'Screech Neck High will get more funding. Screech Neck High will get more funding.' "

A few kids mumbled the words. I sort of whispered them to myself.

"I know it feels silly," Ethan said. "But trust me. Trust the book. Be willing to feel like a jerk at first. It's okay. It's going to work."

He sure was right about the feeling like a jerk part. That aside, I wasn't exactly clear on what school funding had to do with a breaking spork, other than that maybe we should have better eating utensils in the lunchroom, but this didn't seem like the time to ask.

So we all did it, a little louder: "Screech Neck High will get more funding. Screech Neck High will get more funding."

Most of us anyway. I think that big Goth, Landon, was just moving his black-lipsticked lips.

We chanted a few more times, and out of nowhere, the image in my head changed. Instead of breaking, the spork stabbed the french fry, and I was able to pop it into my mouth and eat it.

You know what? It tasted pretty good. Not the best fry I ever ate, but not the worst either.

"Screech Neck High will get more funding. Screech Neck High will get more funding."

Ethan clapped his hands again. "That's it, everyone! That's imanifesting! Get into that state of mind, then you can chant, draw, sing, paint, sculpt, whatever works for you, whatever helps you express your desired reality. If everyone does that just a few minutes a day, by next week, Screech High will be rolling in dough."

Or at least stronger sporks.

That was it for the second meeting. Erica was first out the door. She must have seen me and felt as embarrassed about the chanting as I did. I was starting to feel bad that I hadn't talked to her all this past week, and with things not going so well with Vicky I didn't want to lose my only other friend.

As for Vicky, I knew she was pissed about the way I spoke

to Master Ethan. I was planning to ask her to share an umbrella so we could talk about it, but when I turned around, she wasn't even in her seat.

I hopped up and went to the door, hoping to catch either Vicky or Erica.

Vicky was out in the rain, sloshing her way across the parking lot. I thought about running after her but realized how pathetic that would be.

"See you next meeting," Ethan said, right behind me at the door.

From far off, Vicky turned back and smiled. At him.

I got this pang. Jealousy. Defeat. Both. Weird as Ethan was, there was something about him that seemed pretty cool, and I worried he was better than me. Or at least that he looked better to someone who didn't appreciate my slacker ways.

A few more steps and Vicky vanished into the gray.

The rain came down harder, which made me realize I needed a bathroom, so I headed back into the school. Even with the lights on, the place was dark, and with the students gone, very empty. The slosh of my wet sneakers against the linoleum echoed along the hall.

I walked into the bathroom, pushing in the worn old door. Someone else was there. It was Landon, the guy who wanted an Xbox. He was washing his hands at the sink. Between the rushing water and the rain pelting the window, I guess he hadn't heard me come in and figured he was still alone.

His face was all serious, and he was looking down at his soapy hands, rubbing them, chanting softly to himself,

"Screech Neck High will get more funding. Screech Neck High will get more funding. Screech Neck High will get more funding."

"Right," I thought. "When hell freezes over. When pigs have wings . . .

". . . when Vicky starts seeing me again."

As I left the school, my bus was pulling away from the stop. Rather than stand in the rain another twenty minutes, I booked, my feet slamming puddles, sending water spraying up.

Wait, wait, wait!

But it kept moving.

Wait, wait, wait!

Just for the hell of it, remembering the spork, I tried as hard as I could to imagine the bus stopping for me. All at once, it hissed to a standstill and the doors flopped opened. Just like I'd imagined.

Coincidence. Had to be.

I got on, flashed my pass, paid my quarter, and thanked the man. No seats, of course, but through a sea of backpacks and soggy hair, I caught a glimpse of Erica hunched over her notebook. I ambled over, squeezing between wet umbrellas and coats.

As I got closer, I could see that the skin on her face was wet. Drops of rainwater beaded on that hat of hers. It was a good look.

"Hey," I said.

She looked up. "Hey, stranger. Slouching towards Bethlehem?"

"Huh?"

"Yeats. 'And what rough beast, its hour come round at last, Slouches towards Bethlehem to be born?' "

"I'm a rough beast?"

"No, Mr. Dunne," she said. "But you could stand up straighter."

So I stood up straighter. Some water dripped down my face.

"Rain sucks," I said.

Her brow crinkled. "Odd. I like it."

"Yeah, I could tell by that huge grin on your face," I told her. I nodded at the open notebook in her lap. "Catch-up for all the creative writing classes you've ditched? If I could be any animal in the world . . ."

She shook her head. "No. Algebra."

I leaned in and squinted. "Don't see any numbers."

She turned the book my way. On it, over and over, in her neat, tiny handwriting, it said, "I will ace my algebra class. I will ace my algebra class. I will ace my algebra class."

The words covered the page.

I wanted to ask her if she really believed that junk, but that'd be a pretty stupid question, right? I mean, why fill a page like that if she didn't? So I decided to play along.

"A little *Rule of Won* freelancing?"

"I already did a page of 'Screech Neck High will get more funding,' so I thought I might move on."

I leaned forward and whispered conspiratorially, "I think I may have just gotten the bus to stop for me."

"Maybe . . . but I saw you coming so I shouted to the driver to stop. I can be pretty loud."

"Oh." Made sense. I was surprised to feel a little disappointed. "Thanks. So . . . think that'll help your studying?"

Her brow furrowed as if I'd missed the point. "Study? What for?"

Usually that's *my* line, but math was never a big problem for me. "Are you kidding? Not at all?"

"Non, mon ami, je ne devrais avoir à," she said. *"C'est la Règle."*

"I don't speak Italian."

"French. No, my friend, I shouldn't have to. It's the Rule."

In spite of myself, I was doing that face-scrunching thing big time. Was she pulling my leg? Would I look like an idiot if I believed her?

"Well, maybe, but studying wouldn't . . . hurt, would it?" I sort of stammered it out in a way that reminded me of All-den.

Erica pursed her lips. "Oh, but it does, like a hot stick in the eye. I've studied until I'm blue in the face and gotten nothing. Writing, meditating, I can handle. This is much, much better."

"Well, good luck with that."

"Why, Mr. Dunne, don't you believe?"

I shrugged. I still didn't buy the magic *if you want it, here it is* part, but was it really totally stupid? It brought a bunch of people together, and now they were all at least thinking about the school in a good way.

"Maybe in some cases. For math? I don't know."

"But you've read the book, right?"

I rolled my eyes. "Not yet."

A dark, wry smile crossed her features. "Caleb, why are you in the Crave?"

I blew some air through pursed lips. "To open my horizons?"

"Good. At least you're not just trying to impress some ex-girlfriend who's running for president so you can get back together with her."

My brain shot right past the whole sarcasm thing. "What do you mean, *ex*?"

Erica went back to her writing. The rest of the trip was quiet.

When I got home—home being a one-bedroom apartment in a subsidized housing project, with a dozen locks on the door—the place was empty. It's a little dark here later in the day, but they'd fumigated recently, so at least the roaches were gone. Mom got home from work late so often I was forgetting what she looked like, and Grandpa Joey, well, you never knew whether he'd be around or not. He runs his own auto repair shop in town. Sometimes he'll spend all night working on a car, sometimes, despite his honest streak, he won't show. Drives his customers nuts.

Maybe that's why business wasn't so good.

I cracked some windows to let out the bug-spray stench, then, again for the hell of it, chanted, "Screech Neck High will get more funding" a few times.

It felt stupid, so I started singing it to the tune of "American Idiot" by Green Day. That was kind of fun: "Screechneckhighwillgetmorefunding—dehdehdehdehdehdehdeh."

Even that got tired fast, and I figured I'd done my part for the day. When it didn't work, no one could blame me.

I had no homework, and that damn book was sitting on the table where I'd left it since the previous week, so I picked it up, hopped on the couch, and opened to page one. That wasn't really for the hell of it. I wanted to be able to tell Vicky I'd at least cracked it open, and yeah, by now I was curious. I mean, the thirty million people who bought it couldn't be totally out of their minds, could they? Maybe *some* of it was okay.

I thought Vicky had been making fun of me when she'd said it was an easy read. Nope. Not only were there plenty of pictures, it was also printed on thick paper with huge type, which made the book look a lot longer than it actually was. I also felt like I'd already read most of it, since everything Ethan had said was practically a direct quote.

Yadda-yadda-yadda, people ruin their own lives with negative thoughts, yadda-yadda-yadda, you can have it all, yadda-yadda-yadda, imanifest your mesmories, yadda-yadda-yadda . . .

I was halfway through when a voice called out, "Caleb!"

My heart nearly lurched up into my eyeballs. A short thin figure stood in the bedroom doorway. It was my mother. She's a pretty woman—dark brown hair, dark eyes, a little heavy, but healthy looking. Her retail business suit was so familiar it looked like a second skin.

I'd thought I was alone, but I guess she was napping before her evening shift.

"What, Ma? What?" I shouted as I threw myself into a seated position and made ready to grab her and run out of the apartment. I thought the building was on fire, or she was being attacked by a robber.

She grinned. "You're reading! Guess my hard work really is for something."

I exhaled. "Not if you scare me like that again. Trying to kill me?"

"Sorry, sweetie," she said, and then she came over and mussed my hair. As she did, she looked down at the title and made a face.

"Something wrong?" I asked.

She quickly shook her head. "No. It's just that everyone at work is reading that thing, and I never thought of you as faddish. At least it's got words in it."

"What do you think of it?"

Late for work, she was already edging toward the door. "Can't say. I haven't read it, but it reminds me of something I read when I was your age, *Out on a Limb*, by Shirley MacLaine. All about reincarnation and mysticism."

"Mom," I said, a little annoyed. "I think this is a little more scientific."

"I'm sure it is," she said, but in a way that made me think she was sure it wasn't. I winced inwardly, worried she'd heard my earlier electric-guitar chanting. She smiled and opened the door. "Gotta go, sweetie."

Alone again, I settled back onto the couch and returned to the book. Like I said, it was an easy read, and I cruised through the rest faster than a graphic novel.

I was just about finished, still lying on the sofa, trying to shift so the loose spring wouldn't poke my spine, when the door rattled, and my peace was again disturbed. This time by Grandpa Joey.

He's a gnarled old guy, but gnarled in a way that makes everything about him seem strong, the way a knot in a piece of wood is tougher, denser than the rest. He insists I call him Joey. It's not his name, just the name on the sign of the repair place he bought forty years ago, Joey's Auto Repairs. Since all his customers call him Joey, he tells me he's getting too old to answer to too many names. Mom still calls him Dad.

"What the hell's going on?" he said, slamming his tool case down with a thud. He always dropped it in the same spot. The wood in the floor there was scratched and worn. "The TV isn't on. You sick?"

"No, I'm reading. You're just like Mom. What is it with you guys? I read sometimes."

"Right. And sometimes I like to put on ballet tights and do a few pliés."

I held the book up, to prove what I said was true. He squinted at it.

"What's it about?"

"Positive thinking."

He laughed. "I'm positive you're wasting your time. That

positive enough for you? Why don't you read a Chilton's or something useful?"

"This could be useful," I said. I pretended to go back to reading, even though I was up to the index.

He shook his head and kept walking. A few paces toward the kitchen, he stopped short, then turned around to look at me again.

"It's for some girl, right?"

Joey's still got a lot on the ball.

"Any use lying?" I asked.

"Nah."

"Then yeah. Pretty much."

Chuckling, he came back and patted me on the shoulder, as if he were proud of me and sorry for me at the same time.

That's Joey. I'd like to say he was my father figure if he weren't so much like a freaking lawn gnome with attitude. But I love him nearly the same as I love Mom.

Actually reading the book didn't change my opinion. Believing in *The Rule* still felt like believing in Santa Claus, without the having-to-be-good part. Even so, when I went to bed that night, I thought of my spork and said those words to myself over and over, "Screech Neck High will get more funding."

Might as well, right?

Next morning, when I saw Vicky in the hall, I didn't call to her, I just snuck up and spun her around.

She looked annoyed until I said, "Read it."

"Really?"

"Cover to cover. Even the index. Had no idea how many words start with 'X.'"

"That's great. I'm so proud of you, Caleb," she said.

She got so excited, she gave me a hug, wrapping her arms around me and clicking her painted fingernails together across my shoulders. I think they had little eyeballs on them that day, but they went by so fast, I couldn't be sure. It felt nice, don't get me wrong, but it wasn't exactly a boyfriend/girlfriend hug, more a brother/sister thing.

Sometimes, even when I know what's up, I still go through the motions. It's the downside of being a slacker, I guess, not being willing to change direction unless you absolutely have to, because it requires effort.

"So, can we go out again sometime?"

She froze, face still smiling, only now she wasn't smiling because she was happy, more like she was buying time.

"Sure," she finally said.

Then there was an even *bigger* pause.

"Maybe we can get together with some of the kids from the Crave," she said.

"That's not exactly what I had in—"

She kept going, like I hadn't even opened my mouth. "Isn't the book amazing? Isn't Ethan amazing? I mean, he really understands, and he really believes. You can just see it in his eyes, and he talks like he's on fire."

"Yeah," I said. "And did you check out his shoelaces?"

Instead of responding, she kept talking. I nodded a whole lot until Vicky said she had to go do something or other and I said I had to do something or other, too, so I trudged off, all but convinced we had just broken up.

I was heading toward trig when I spotted All-den struggling to stuff books into his overpacked locker. This guy was always stuffing things, grunting and shoving, just like a cartoon character.

I scooped up a few and held them out to him.

"Caleb," he said.

"All-den," I answered.

We stood there a second, me holding out the books, him unable to grab them because he couldn't move his hands. He nodded toward the pile he was holding up. I rolled my eyes and moved in.

I shoved the books I was holding on top of the pile, then held the whole mess in place as he slammed the locker shut.

"Why do you have all this stuff anyway?"

"I'm the editor of the paper," he mumbled. "It's . . . research."

"Right," I said. "I heard about the editor thing. Congratulations. What are you researching?"

His eyes shifted around. "Nothing."

"No, what?"

He looked at his locker door. "Actually, I've been checking over police and construction reports, trying to prove you were responsible for the vandalism that brought the gym down."

I shook my head. "Great. That's just . . . terrific, really. Thank you *so* much."

Finally, All-den got himself enough together to look me in the eye. It was weird. His eyes, I mean. They were this bright green. Then he said the magic words: "Near as I can tell so far, you had nothing to do with it."

My eyes lit up. "Really?" I asked.

All-den nodded slowly. "The construction company was using the original school blueprints, which, it turns out, have a design flaw that caused the gym to collapse during the storm in the first place and . . . probably caused the second collapse, too."

"Great! That's just . . . terrific! Really! Thank you *so* much!" I said. "Going to write an article on it?"

"I suppose I should. Yes."

I could've hugged the guy. "All-den, you are one okay dude!"

"Please, call me Moore."

"Why?"

"I don't like the way you say All-den."

"Fine, Moore. Everyone's going to know. Funny, it's just like . . ."

"What?"

"Well, it's like what I asked for in my Crave."

I couldn't believe I actually said that out loud. Neither could All-den, or Moore, or whoever he was.

He tsked loudly. "Freaking Vanuatu."

"I am not a freaking . . . what?"

"Vanuatu. *Mondo Cane.*"

"I don't speak Italian."

"It's not Italian. It's from a movie."

"What's it mean?"

"Look it up."

I was about to explain how totally unlikely *that* was when a shrieking Vicky rushed up.

"Did you hear? Did you hear?" She was so loud, everyone in the hall turned to stare.

"What?"

"It worked!" she shouted. "It worked! Screech Neck High just got a grant for, like, half a million dollars! They're going to rebuild the gym!"

I broke out in a huge grin.

"Really?"

"Really!"

"Ha!" I said. I turned to All-den—I mean Moore—and said, "Ha!"

He shook his head. I turned back to Vicky and we just stood there, wordless, grinning, shaking with excitement.

It worked!

Out of nowhere, her body was up against mine, and not like a brother and sister. This time our lips pressed together. I think she may have meant to just hug me but was so excited, she forgot where to stop.

Me? I pushed forward and opened my mouth a little. Maybe it was just out of old habit, but she, as they say, reciprocated.

And man, no matter what All-den Moore had to say about the Vana-whatsis, did I ever love *The Rule of Won* just then.

- I would still like the greatest gaming system in the world, the Xbox. A 733 MHz Intel main processor and 233 MHz graphics processor from nVidia create photorealistic graphics in real time. A huge hard drive stores saved games and characters, and a built-in Ethernet port enables super-fast multiplayer online gaming over a broadband Internet connection. —Landon

- Freaky about the funding. Some other stuff happened this week, too, not ten million dollars, which I was just kidding about, but I was thinking a few days ago how much I loved my mother's apple crisp and how she never makes it anymore, and out of nowhere we had some after dinner. I'm starting to think this is pretty cool. There's stuff I want for myself, too, but I'm not sure where to start, so this time, I think I'm just going to sit back and see what happens next. —Dylan

- Our lame-ass basketball team sucks. Yeah, we don't have our own gym to practice in, but we haven't won a game in ages.

We're the laughingstock of the state, a joke to the world and ourselves. So what say we picture the Basket Cases kicking some serious ass for a change? —Mike

- Forget the spider strength. I'll get real. How about the school uses some of that money for a new swimming pool? —Jacob

- I'd like my grandfather's auto repair shop to start making more money so we can start to pay off our credit card debt. He's a smart, hardworking guy, the best in town with a diesel engine, but the customers don't show up anymore. He says it's the economy, but I'm thinking it feels more like bad luck. —Caleb

- Oh, algebra! Once you were the grim steel lock on the fast iron door of my dreams, but I will open you! Once you were the hairy wild beast, all red teeth and yellow eyes, that threatened to shred my poor soul, but I will tame you! Once you were forever beyond my reach, as far as the stars, but I will grasp you! I will ace this freaking class! I will! I will! I will! —Erica

- Of course I still want to win the election, but it almost seems selfish to think of that now. We have a real chance to change things around here. We've proved it! We have the power! I hope everyone, in the Crave and the school, starts to take part in our student government so we can all work together and make this place as great as I know it can be! —Vicky

- I knew it! I knew it! I knew it! Of COURSE the book works! I wrote to Jasper Trelawney the minute I found out about the grant, and he posted the message at his Web site! It's one of about a trillion, and he hasn't written back yet, but I know he will, because it's what I really want! —Grace

- I suggested the money for the school, and I was very excited when we got it, but now it feels like there's something creepy about the whole thing. I mean, I guess it could just be a coincidence, but if it isn't, I'm a little worried what might happen if we ask for the wrong things. Maybe I'm just not ready to have whatever I want, or maybe I don't think I deserve it, or whatever, but I think I'm just going to sit this round out and let someone else come up with something worthy to wish for. —Dana

- Whoa! We got our funding AND my parents caved and decided to let me stay home alone while they're out of town! I'm going to throw a little get-together, nothing big. Vicky, maybe we can celebrate your election? I know it's going to happen! My wish? One freaking fantastic vacation! —Jane

- This is my first time. I'm not exactly shy, but no matter how much time I spend dressing up or trying to talk to people, I never seem to be as popular as some of the other girls. Just for once, I'd like it to be me everyone says hello to. —Olivia

- I'm glad there's finally a place in this school where we can talk about spiritual issues with each other. I know how hard it can be, especially when a lot of the other kids think it's not cool to believe in something. The three things I want for myself are the courage to change the things I can, the patience to accept the things I can't change, and the wisdom to know the difference. —Will

- I don't know if this is the sort of thing you're supposed to ask for, but there's this hot girl in my astronomy class I just can't stop thinking about. It's not love or anything. More of a magnificent obsession. I'd kill for a chance with her, so, yeah, I'm happy to chant or whatever. —Jeff

- I managed to find my slate tank top on eBay. No real magic, but just the same, thanks. What I'm feeling like now are some shoes to match. —Beth

- After I found out about the money, I pulled myself together, broke those sacred clique lines, and talked to that guy. I pretended I could hear what was playing on his earbuds and told him I liked it. He actually shared an earbud with me, and we're meeting tomorrow in study hall. What I want is for this to keep going the way it's going! —Kathleen

- I would love for my mother to get a freaking raise, so she can take some time off from work and be home with Angie, my little sister. I have to be home all the time and have, like, no social life. Mom's up for review next week, so, please? —Hailey

- Last year my father's store was robbed. He had a shotgun shoved in his face. It really scared the crap out of me and I'm still on anti-anxiety meds. I used to feel okay at school, but lately I've been having nightmares about this creepy guy I see in the lunchroom coming into class and shooting everyone. I try to run, but it's like my feet are stuck in molasses. For all I know, he's an okay guy, but I want the dreams to stop. —Lauren

- Despite all my personal imanifesting, Nicole's iPhone has not broken yet. Someone on the revenge.net message board told me maybe I was feeling conflicted about this, like maybe I didn't want to hurt Nicole, but that's ridiculous. Another person said maybe I should be more specific, and that made sense. So maybe one of those metal detectors could go on the fluke as she passed through it, creating a big emf blast that would wipe the iPhone clean? —Sophia

Happiness is one of those things you can spend days trying to describe, weeks wishing for, years trying to find, but when it finally washes over you in one big fat wave, you still have no idea what it is. You just grab on, ride the feeling, and hope to hell it lasts, even though you know deep down things couldn't possibly be this good forever.

In the dizzy days that followed I wore my button proudly, posted my Crave without fear, waved to fellow Cravers in the halls, and pitied any who led a lesser life. And oh, yeah, though Vicky still pulled me into a corner away from everyone whenever we met, now it was for swapping spit.

A little spork, a little chanting, and the world lay at my feet. I daily thanked the ancient Greeks, the gods of Slackerdom, and yes, *The Rule of Won*.

Because, I mean, who *wouldn't* believe after that?

It was Wednesday morning, the day of our first Crave since the announcement. I'd woken up two hours early, all jazzed, so I finished up some homework, then, figuring I'd crash in school if I didn't get some sleep, decided to snooze on our crappy couch until it was time to leave for the bus. I was feeling great despite the broken spring poking my back, thinking of Vicky's lips against mine, about to slip off, when . . . *wham*!

Something hit me on the side of the head.

"*What?*"

I sprang up and looked around. Joey was next to me, a rolled-up newspaper in his gnarled hands.

"What are you smiling about?" he croaked.

"I'm happy! I'm smiling! What, it's against the law?"

He shook the paper at me like it was a loaded gun. "Since when do you care about the law? Remember when the cops came for you? You're up to something."

"I'm not! I swear! Things are just going good, you know? And someone's doing an article about how I had nothing to do with the gym. It was crappy construction!"

He narrowed his eyes. "Maybe, but you're smiling too much. Something's bound to go wrong."

"Like someone smacking me in the head while I'm trying to nap?"

"Worse."

"Geez, Joey," I said. "Y'ever stop to think maybe things keep going wrong around here because you *expect* them to?"

He hit me with the paper again.

"Ow!"

"You expect that?"

"No, but . . ."

"There you go."

"I swear, Joey," I mumbled, shaking my head.

"Fine. Just don't swear in front of me or your mother."

"Very funny."

"Yeah, it was, thanks. Just remember not to keep your head in the clouds too long or you'll trip and wind up on your butt in an alley with a new tattoo on your arm."

He wandered into the kitchen, cackling.

I guess he was trying to say, in his special GP Joey way, that I shouldn't get too carried away. Either that or maybe he was going into that second childhood thing and just liked hitting people. Sometimes he's like a wrinkled version of that wise-man mandrill from *The Lion King,* Rafiki. Sometimes he's just nuts.

Speaking of lovable nuts, even the dark Erica had lightened considerably. On the bus that morning, she didn't even quote a poem about death or suicide. When I said hello, she said, Hey, like she was normal.

I was thinking of kidding her about her good mood, but figured that would make me too much like Joey with the newspaper. If she was still happy in a week or so, I'd rib her then. She did seem a little nonplussed when I talked about how well Vicky and I were getting along, but I had no idea why.

Fencing soon went up around the new construction site, and our beloved Dr. Wyatt could be seen spending a lot of QT with muscular dudes in hard hats. Even he didn't glare at me lately. Maybe it was because he'd read that police report

All-den Moore—just Moore now by request—talked about. Oh, *everyone* didn't love me—the school newspaper hadn't come out yet—but with all the excitement, they were forgetting they hated me.

Looking up, you tend to notice more things. For instance, I noticed the aforementioned Moore again between second and third period, and for a change, he wasn't stuffing papers into something, and he wasn't alone. He was with three other people, a girl and two guys. All of them looked sort of familiar, but I couldn't place them. They were all headed out of the student newspaper office, walking in formation, following Moore's lead.

I figured I could use the occasion to ask when the article was coming out, and maybe find out what the hell "Vanuatu" meant without having to lift a finger.

"Moore!" I called.

They all stopped, like a well-oiled machine. Well, maybe not a *well-oiled* machine, heck, maybe not even a machine, but they all stopped.

"Got yourself a posse?" I said cheerfully. I was saying everything cheerfully these days.

Seeing my pin, one of them, a square kind of guy built sort of like a short door, except with more fat than muscle, moved to block me from getting closer. He was wearing a trench coat.

"It's okay," Moore told him, raising his hand like he might have to hold him back.

"You sure?" he said.

Moore nodded and the square man relaxed a bit, but the

other two—a lean, anxious, lanky guy in a dirty white T-shirt and denim vest who was crouching as if the ceiling were right above him, and a well-dressed brunette girl with braces, freckles, and a predatory look—kept giving me the evil eye.

"My staff: Guy, Drik, and Mason," Moore said, pointing, in turn, to Square Man, the lanky scared kid, and the mean-looking girl.

That's when I recognized them. I'd known them all since grade school. All three were kids everyone had picked on, only now they were better dressed, almost cool looking, and they were together, like they were getting organized. Despite the mouth breathing and the braces, Mason's hair, for instance, cupped her face nicely, making her look kind of pretty.

I'd never gone in big for the picking-on thing myself. That jock Dylan from the Crave and a couple of his pals used to, but I think even they grew out of it.

"So when's the *Weekly Screech* coming out? And, if I may be so bold, the article that clears me?"

"We changed the name," Guy said curtly, as if I should know. "It's *The Otus* now."

"*Otus* is the genus that the screech owl belongs to," Mason, the girl, chimed in.

"Changed some other things, too," the tall guy, Drik, said in a quiet voice. He seemed to be talking more to my pin than me. "We're getting serious. For starters we're doing a big exposé of *The Rule of Won*."

I laughed. "What are you going to expose? You have to admit we've had pretty good results."

Moore laughed back, through his nose. "You really think your club got the school that grant by wishing for it really hard?"

"Well . . . yeah," I said. Moore had a way of talking sometimes that was so arrogant, if he'd said, "You really think your name's Caleb?" I'd have to wonder about that, too.

He snapped his fingers. Mason slapped a sheet of paper into his hands, which Moore held out to me for inspection. It was a photocopy of an article from the local paper, with the headline "Screech Neck High Up for Grant."

Moore pointed at the date. "Printed last month. The National Zetetic Foundation had to award a substantial sum of money to some school, or they'd be in danger of losing their tax-exempt status. The chairman is an SNH graduate. Dana Krull probably read the same article, which made her think of her Crave. Ethan Skinson may have read it, too, which made him pick it. Not really so magic when the odds are stacked like that, is it?"

"Oh, please," I said. "You're just trying to . . . hey, how did you know it was Dana's Crave or that Ethan picked it?"

While his posse looked around nervously, Moore blinked. "We're reporters."

"Well, big deal." I tossed the paper back at him. "The final decision wasn't made yet, so we still could have had something to do with that."

Also on the plus side for *The Rule* was the fact that Moore himself was going to clear me, people liked me again, and Vicky and I were back together.

Moore shook his head like he felt sorry for me. "You know what circular reasoning is, Caleb? Begging the question?"

"Of course I do. Uh . . . is it like Vanuatu?"

Sour-faced Mason stepped up again. "No, it means once you assume something is true, you can't use reason to disprove it. As long as you believe you caused the school to get the grant, you'll take any data and twist it around to match that assumption."

I puffed my chest up defensively. "Ha! I will *not* take any assumption and . . . and . . . do what you said with it."

"Right," Moore said. He waved his little gang forward. They fell back into their marching order.

"Hey," I called after them. "Still doing that article about the construction, right?"

They didn't answer. My heart sank a little. If Moore was anything like the previous editors, there might not even be an issue until the week before summer vacation.

Still, I wasn't going to let their snippy cracks about *The Rule* shake my new faith, especially since I didn't particularly understand them.

This time at the meeting, everyone came back. We even had a few new faces, making our trailer feel a little crowded. A few of the quieter kids like Landon seemed livelier. Some had even bought themselves "1" pins. The mood was so good, I soon found myself thinking that Moore and his pals were just losers.

Vicky sat next to me, hot red and orange flames adorning her fingernails. I pulled her chair closer and wrapped my arm around her waist. I think Erica picked her head up for a second from her writing to watch, but it was hard to tell.

Ethan was bubbly himself, clapping his hands together even more than last time. Before he could get the Crave started, Vicky applauded. Everyone joined in. A few of us, myself among them, hooted.

"So far so good, right?" he said.

The applause grew louder. Ethan got that mad scientist twinkle in his eyes. Before the clapping faded, he raised his voice. "We're just getting warmed up. Now we're going to do some heavy-duty imanifesting for our basketball team so they break their losing streak and kick the Regis High Hurricanes' asses next week!"

Mike clenched his right hand, swiped it in the air, and said, "Yes!"

Everyone applauded again. Good times.

Then Ethan went into his thing about mesmories and imanifesting to catch up the newcomers, and we all chanted about how the Basket Cases would win their next game. I don't know if it was the breathing or just the overall high feeling, but I conjured my spork easily and kept seeing it fly into a basket.

When we chanted, pretty much everyone put something into it, and it really did feel like we all shared one great big Voice.

I wondered if I should tell anyone about that article Moore was planning, but I decided, the same way I decided to leave Erica's new smile alone, to let it sit. I wanted to ask Vicky out after the meeting, and I had a feeling that if I didn't do anything stupid, she'd say yes. So I didn't do anything stupid. Besides, the Hurricanes were a great team and our guys didn't even have a gym. If we could pull that off, what question could there be in *anyone's* mind?

When Ethan was finished and everyone rose from their seats, I turned to Vicky, nonchalant as could be, and said, "Coffee?"

"Great!" she said, smiling. "Mind if we ask Ethan to come along?"

I felt like Joey's newspaper had whacked me again.

"Him? Mr. Skinson?"

"Yeah, wouldn't it be nice? He runs the club and everything, but no one hangs out with him. He could use some friends."

"Uh . . ."

Before I could make up some reason to say no, she called out, "Ethan!"

And of course he turned around, Ethan being his name and all.

"I'm sure he's busy," I mumbled to her, but she ignored me.

"Caleb and I are going to Java Jive for some coffee. Want to come with?"

I conjured my spork and thought, "Make him say no, make him say no."

But I guess I wasn't fast enough, because the smile on his face widened.

"Thanks," he said. "That'd be great."

Perfect. A dream come true. Sharing my first date with my girl in ages with the school's brand-new alpha male.

I noticed Erica snickering as she left the trailer, and made a mental note to severely mock her newfound joy the next time I saw her.

The three of us, Ethan, Vicky, and yours truly, headed out across the beautiful asphalt parking lot together, me trying to figure out who the third wheel was, Ethan or me. He and I being guys, we didn't have much to say to each other, but Vicky walked between us, chattering like crazy.

"I just figured that we all know you, but we don't really know you, you know?" she said.

Ethan nodded like he understood, which put him one up on me.

"Maybe next time we should ask the rest of the Crave along," he said.

"Yes," I said, hoping I didn't sound too stiff. "A crowd would be much better."

I casually put my arm around Vicky's waist, but by the time we reached the street, she had managed to quietly shake it free.

As we approached the storefront with the hand-painted sign, Ethan asked, "So how is this place?"

"It's called Java Jive for a reason," Vicky said. "Because the java is, well . . . jive, as in bogus."

"It's not that bad," I said, feeling kind of offended for the poor little store. But Ethan's smile vanished when he saw the vending machine that dished out the coffee. I think he'd pictured more a Starbucks kind of deal.

"Crappacino," he said.

Any luck and maybe he'd hate it so much, he'd leave. Trying to be friendly, I nudged him. "It tastes better if you pour half off and put in lots of sugar. Well, at least then it tastes like sugar."

We got our lousy drinks, mopped up a table with some napkins, and sat. Vicky nudged me a few times to get me to say something, but really, I didn't have anything I wanted to say. This left her to get the conversation rolling, which I have to admit, she did pretty well.

"I know Caleb and I were . . . pretty happy when we heard about the grant, but what did it feel like when you found out? I mean, you began the Crave."

Ethan smiled. He wasn't looking at me or Vicky but at some invisible point off in the distance. "What did it feel like? It felt like being the Eagle of Hell."

"Okay," I said. "And this means?"

He tightened his face and then relaxed it. "Near the academy I used to attend there was this old amusement park, Happy Planet."

"I remember that place," Vicky said. "They shut it down when a little girl died on one of the rides. She unbuckled herself and stood up on the Whirl-A-Gig."

Ethan nodded. "RideCo, a huge corporation, bought up the property and planned to reopen it. While they were fixing it up, we used to sneak in and hang out at the arcade. There was this old machine that still worked for a dime. It tested your strength by giving you a shock when you held on to this metal grip. It'd score you depending on how much of a jolt you could take. The bottom level was Old Lady, the top Eagle of Hell."

"Shock?" I asked. "Like with electricity?"

"Yeah," Ethan said, getting excited. "I think it was broken, or they didn't have safety regulations when the thing was built. It felt like this wild vibration, starting in my thumb, then my hand, elbow, arm, shoulder, even my chest, until my whole body felt shot through with the juice. But I held on until I reached the eagle. I was the only one who ever did that. That's what it felt like when we got that grant, reaching the eagle."

He clenched and unclenched his hands a few times. "My palm had these red marks on them for a week," he said with a laugh.

"Wow," Vicky said.

I couldn't figure out if she was impressed or just weirded out like I was.

"Geez, Ethan," I said. "Some people might think it's kind of stupid to hang on to something that's hurting you."

He twisted his head sideways and toward me, then said, "That depends on what you get if you do, Caleb."

Trying to look cool, he picked up his coffee and knocked some back, but I guess it was even worse than he expected. He gagged.

"You okay?" Vicky said, reaching over and patting him on the back.

"Fine," he said between coughs. She stopped patting and started rubbing him, giving him a little massage. I may have just been imagining that, but I was seething with jealousy.

Still coughing, Ethan reached into his backpack and pulled out a handkerchief. As he did, his hand snagged a sheet of paper that fell out and went sliding across the floor. I'm all about picking up other people's papers, Moore's or Ethan's, so while he finished hacking, I snatched it up and happened to give it a look.

It was a drawing of the school. Not the way it looked now, more the way it might look if it got all fixed up. There was even a new garden on the side. It looked professional, but done in an old sketchy style. I was impressed, even if Ethan was stealing my girl.

"You do this?" I asked.

Vicky leaned over. "That's amazing," she said.

Ethan half smiled. "Yes, it's great. But it's not mine. My sister, Alyssa."

"But it's a picture of our Crave," I said.

"Yep. Alyssa . . . wanted to help out."

"Is she at Screech Neck Middle School?" Vicky asked.

He shook his head. "Dad's homeschooling her." He pursed his lips as he added, "One reason he's not making as much money as he used to, but that's the way it has to be, I guess. She . . . uh . . . she just doesn't do anything anyone tells her if it doesn't make sense to her, and you never know what's going to make sense to her. Hell, Parker Academy barely knew what to do with her. One week in a public school and they'd diagnose her as ADD, ADHD, OCD, autistic, Asperger's, or schiz. And she's none of those things, she's just . . . Alyssa."

Ethan reached for the drawing, so I handed it back.

"Nice work," I said. "Kind of an old style."

He shrugged as he slipped it into his backpack. "She made it look like a Blake etching, like the proverbs on the back of my door."

"Why?"

"To have a little fun with me, I think. It's how my mother used to draw sometimes. I got my dad's brains, Alyssa inherited Mom's . . . talent. She's got a weird sense of humor that's all her own, though."

Vicky leaned forward and took Ethan's hands in hers.

I was like, *Hello, I am still in the room here!*

"You sound like you worry about her."

He shook his head. "She worries more about me than I do about her. Funny kid. I don't think she understands the sheer power she . . . I mean, *everyone* has. How many things it could fix for her."

"You mean from *The Rule*?" Vicky offered.

He looked at her like he was only half listening, then nodded.

"So . . . Ethan . . . ," I said, watching Vicky's hands on his. "That girl on the ride at Happy Planet. *The Rule* says if it happened, she must have wanted it to happen, right?"

"Yes."

"I don't get that. You think she wanted to die?"

"Caleb?" Vicky said.

As far as I was concerned, I wasn't trying to trip him up. It was just an honest question.

He made a face. "She crawled out from the harness, didn't she? Did she understand what would happen? She was eight, not two. She was in a spinning ride going about fifty miles an hour. How could some part of her not?"

"But why would anyone want to die like that?"

"Who knows? Maybe part of her knew she had something like a brain tumor that hadn't been discovered yet and she wanted a quick death instead of a slow one. Maybe she was being abused and didn't want to live at all. Maybe part of her knew the ride was going to collapse the next week and hurt a lot of people and this was the only way to save them. I mean, would you rather believe she died for something or died for nothing?"

I'd never really thought of it as my choice, but he did sort of make a kind of sense. Didn't he?

After a respectful silence, I said, "Ethan, do you know what 'Vanuatu' means?"

"No," he said. "What?"

"Never mind."

"Erica?"

"Who's calling?"

"Caleb."

"Mr. Caleb Dunne? The quintessential slacker? Has he actually picked up a phone?"

"Yeah."

"Unprecedented. What's up?"

"Uh . . . you going to the game Saturday?"

"Maybe. It's a toss-up between that and putting a spike through my head."

"Then may I suggest that the basketball game would be the slightly better choice?"

"How so?"

"There's popcorn, for instance. And . . . I . . . thought maybe you could come with us."

"*Us?*"

"Me and Vicky . . . and Ethan."

"Aha. Now *that* sounds much more fun to watch than some

silly old basketball game. Pay for the popcorn and you can count me in."

"Good. I think. Pick you up at six?"

"I'll be waiting, my heart aflutter."

"Uh . . . okay. Bye."

I hung up, then rapped the phone against my forehead a few times, trying to imagine that spike through my head. Erica saying yes somehow made our new group date more real. I should have seen it coming, but when I asked Vicky to the game, it was just like the coffee shop—why don't we ask Ethan along? Right. Why don't we carry him there? Why don't we build a little hutch for him, so we can feed him and keep him warm? Isn't Ethan great? Why can't you be more like Ethan? Why can't *everyone* be more like Ethan? That way, whenever I looked at someone, I could see Ethan.

I felt stupid for hating the guy. I should be angry with Vicky. Unless Ethan was secretly trying to imanifest her away from me. Why not? I thought about using *The Rule* to win her back. I pictured me and Ethan as Voldemort and Harry Potter, squaring off with our wands. Well, Ethan would have a wand. I'd have a spork. And I'm not totally sure which of us would be Voldemort and which Harry Potter.

After an hour lecture on just how much pressure to put on the brakes, Joey lent me his van, then warned me to keep my nose clean, whatever that meant. I picked up Vicky first, so she'd wind up in the front, next to me, but as soon as we reached Ethan's ranch house, she climbed into the back anyway.

He looked at the old oily interior and wrinkled his nose a bit. I don't think it was a money thing, like he was too good to get in, more like he was afraid of dirt. Somehow he managed, and of course Vicky stayed in back with him. She did look a little annoyed when Erica got in the front, next to me, and that pleased me a bit.

Regis, the town where the game was taking place, was a good forty-minute drive. The muffler on the van was shot and the interior acted like a big drum, so when I hit the highway and took it over forty, it was too loud to talk to anyone except whoever was right next to you. In the rearview mirror I could see Vicky and Ethan chatting merrily away. I turned to Erica, and there she was, of course, writing in her journal.

"That thing stitched to your hand?" I asked her.

"Yes," she said vacantly. "The staples hurt too much."

I wound up mostly keeping my eyes on the road.

After we parked, which was easy at Regis compared with SNH, Ethan hopped out and looked down at his pants, worried.

"Damn. I've got some kind of stain."

I didn't see anything myself, but hey, I don't bleach my shoelaces either.

"You know where the bathroom is here?" he asked.

Vicky half climbed out and sort of posed. She was dressed to kill in a tight orange sweater and short skirt. Her fingernails had little basketballs on them. It was kind of retro for her, but she looked terrific. "Why don't you show him, Caleb? Erica and I will get seats and see if anyone else from the Crave is here yet."

"Fine," I mumbled, and I led super-cool Ethan to the john.

Regis High School was Ethan to my Screech Neck. It was a newer, bigger structure with porcelain-sided brown brick and visible steel girders that gave it a twenty-first-century gleam. It was more brightly lit and had much nicer vending machines. The huge gym, nearly a separate building, had these neat bleachers that folded straight into nooks in the walls. Ethan nodded with approval as we made our way to the sparkling bathroom, where all the stalls had doors and the tiles gave off a minty fresh odor.

As we went in, two guys in Regis Hurricane uniforms were exiting. They were stooped, slouching so much that I, at five eight, was nearly as tall as they. Their hanging faces looked white and sweaty, as if they'd seen a ghost or been puking their guts out. Turned out to be what Mrs. D would call the latter.

Another Regis kid was behind them, but giving them a wide berth, like they were lepers, so I said to him, "Hey, they looked sick."

He nodded. "Stomach flu. Half the team and most of the school's got it. Our best players are on the sidelines, and I think we just lost two more. No offense, man, but if they were playing any other school, they'd just cancel the game."

"None taken," I said.

He left. Ethan and I looked at each other. The game hadn't even begun and already the odds were stacked in our favor. It felt good for a second, giddy, but then . . . it just didn't. I mean, how good can you feel about people puking?

Ethan didn't have a problem. "*The Rule* works in weird

ways," he said as he walked over to the sink. He wet a paper towel and rubbed it against that invisible stain on his pants.

"It's . . . kinda freaky, isn't it?" I said. "Makes you wonder—what if someone got really hurt making one of our dreams come true?"

He stopped rubbing, that mad scientist glint flashing. "Don't go there, Caleb. Everyone gets only what they ask for. If these guys have the flu, if they lose, or even if a building falls on them, it's because they wanted it that way."

The look vanished, and he smiled. "But I understand. It's easy to have doubts."

"You don't seem to have any."

"Nope," he said. He went back to his cleaning. "Except maybe whether this stain will come out or not."

You have to understand, I hated the guy because Vicky liked him, but, unlike Moore, who just annoyed me whether he was right or wrong, Ethan had this air of calm authority I respected and, well, feared a little. Part of me believed he *did* have all the answers.

"Hey, Ethan, can I ask you something?"

"Sure."

"Rumor is your dad lost his job and the house."

He raised an eyebrow. "And you're wondering why I just don't imanifest more money for myself and my family, get back what we lost?"

"Well, yeah. Why don't you?"

Hearing it out loud, I felt stupid for asking, like I'd just asked a priest, if God was all-powerful, could he make a rock so big he himself couldn't lift it? That always struck me as a good question, but it was an insulting one, one a kid would ask.

Ethan buffed the paper towels against his pants like he was shining shoes.

"Well, Caleb, the human mind's a funny thing," he began, which made me feel even more like an idiot. "We think of all sorts of things. Millions of thoughts a minute. The thoughts we're aware of are just the tip of an iceberg. Can't control *all* of them, right? I'm sure everything in my life happened because part of me wanted it to, but I can't be sure why. I think it happened maybe because it was part of my bigger purpose."

My mind flashed back to the day the gym collapsed. Had I been there for a reason? *Was* I secretly ashamed of being a slacker?

"I don't get it. You think you're subconsciously punishing yourself?"

He folded the paper towel in fours, tossed it out, and straightened his pant leg. "No. No, no, no. I think maybe I sent myself here to help out people like you, who really need it. I mean, look around. Who needs help more than Screech Neck? Some of you guys don't even have cell phones."

He had on this half grin that might've been sheepish, but if you looked at it another way, it was smug. If he was trying to joke with me, I wasn't laughing.

"Cell phones?"

The grin got wider. Smug. Definitely smug now. "Sure, you act like it's okay, but it's like you're not part of the twenty-first century. If you ask the kids what college they want to go to, most don't even know. And that's the *seniors*. I mean, unless you have some idea of what you want to do with your life, you'll never do anything, right, Caleb?"

"Right."

Only . . . my ambition is to float.

He slapped me on the shoulder on his way out. "If I'm here talking to you, you must have wanted me here for some reason, too. Maybe I'm here to help fix everybody."

I had another question, but the door closed behind him.

I asked anyway, to myself, "Dude, are you sure we're broken?"

I stepped out in the hall and made my way toward the gym. There weren't many people around. There never were when the Basket Cases played, but even so, this crowd was anemic. Searching for snacks, I spotted a nice old-fashioned corn popper in a red wagon in front of the gym doors. Even their freaking popcorn was special. Remembering my deal with Erica, I plopped down four bucks for two bags.

As I reached the gym doors, which, of course, are these beautiful polished things that made you feel like you were entering the Emerald City from Oz, I spotted a familiar figure at the school entrance. It took me a while to realize who it was, because he wasn't dressed in black and didn't have undead eyes or black lips. Still, that size and shape could belong to only one man: Landon, the Goth who craved an Xbox, which sounds kind of like the title of a fairy tale.

Only now, he was wearing tan pants and a blue hoodie. Turns out his hair wasn't even black, it was kind of a sandy brown.

The only reason I recognized him at all was because he was standing next to Screech Neck's remaining Goth contingent, both of them. They'd obviously just arrived and were as surprised as I was by Landon's appearance. As I watched the odd scene unfold, I absently tossed some popcorn into my mouth, surprised by how good it was.

The one with spiked hair and a safety pin through his ear stated the obvious. "Landon, you look like a freaking sun worshipper. This a joke?"

"I thought we were coming to goof on this lame-ass game," the short thin one said. He had stringy bleached-blond hair and was decked out in black leather pants and button-down shirt (I didn't even know they made black leather button-down shirts). His clothes were so tight, you could see his bones poking out. I had no idea how he breathed, or even if he was breathing.

Landon glanced nervously around, then sighed. "I can't do it anymore, Dingo. My Crave is here."

Dingo wasn't buying. "Is this about that stupid *F*-box? You kidding me? Put in your contacts and get some lipstick on. You look like an idiot."

Landon took a lumbering step, as if ready to do as asked, but he stopped abruptly and waved his meaty hands in the air. "No, no. I . . . I have to be true to myself. I have to support the team. I have to support the Crave."

"Landon?! What are you . . ."

He took a step away from them.

Dingo's eyes went from wide to angry to disgusted. "Fine. Screw it. And screw you, Landon."

"Dingo . . ."

Dingo turned his back. "That's it for you, man. That's it. Enjoy your weird-ass book club. Come on, Rad, let's go rent some DVDs and crash in your basement."

Rad, the little bony one, shook his head sadly at Landon, then turned his back.

Landon stood there like an open wound, watching them leave.

Ethan would probably say this was a good thing. Landon was getting rid of the negative elements in his life so he could devote more time to *The Rule of Won*. Landon's parents, thrilled to see their boy's "handsome face" again, would probably agree.

Me, I wasn't so sure. He looked like a big lost puppy dog.

I stepped out. "Hey, Landon."

He half nodded, but didn't speak as I stood beside him. We both watched Rad and Dingo as the glistening doors of the Emerald City closed behind them.

Still chomping on some popcorn, I looked up at the big guy. "I know I don't know you well, Landon, but ever since I first saw you at school you hung out with those guys. How long you known them?"

"Since grade school," he said wistfully.

"Yeah, well . . . ," I said. That's what I say when I don't know what to say. "I'm here with Vicky, Ethan, and Erica. Want to come hang with us?"

"Okay," he said quietly. I held out the popcorn bag and

shook it. He held out his hands and I poured a good serving out. Truth was, he still looked weird in that hoodie. It was at least a size too small. I guess he didn't have many non-Goth clothes to pick from. Still, he was a big guy, and people made a respectful path for us as we walked into the gym.

With Regis flu-ridden and Screech Neck having all the school spirit of a slug, most of the seats were empty and some of the kids in the audience had stretched out across a few, planning to watch the game lying down, I guess. It was easy to spot Erica, way up in the back row. No sense in waving at her, her book was out on her lap as she wrote. Dylan was up there with her, looking all fidgety. Grace the groupie was next to him, bubbling with excitement. She saw me and nearly stood up as she waved at us.

"Over here! Over here!" she shouted, and it, like, echoed through the gym.

But where was Vicky?

As I led Landon across the shiny scuff-free gym floor, I noticed that in the thin alley between the raised seats and the wall there were two figures standing close.

Landon, looking where I was looking, said, "That Ethan?" He nodded toward the taller shadow. "Looks like he's kissing some girl."

I heard Vicky's voice saying, "Ooooooh," like she was feeling faint.

Forgetting Landon, I dove into the little alley. This was awkward, since I was wider than it and had to shimmy sideways.

Vicky saw me and practically leaped away from Ethan. Not easy to do in that tiny space. She nearly smacked her head against the seats in an effort to put some distance between herself and Ethan.

"Caleb!" she said. "I was . . . Ethan was . . ."

Ethan cleared his throat. "I was just showing her the drawing Alyssa did for the game tonight."

I bet he was.

Vicky grinned. "Yeah, I was being a real nag about it."

I bet she was.

"I was just so impressed," she added. She lifted a sheet from Ethan's hands and held it toward me. "It's beautiful, don't you think?"

I didn't take it, what with my hands holding two popcorn bags, but I looked at it, since that was much easier than, say, dealing with whatever Vicky and Ethan were really doing back here. And what was I going to do about it, really? Hit Ethan? Punch Vicky? Burst into tears?

At least I had the picture to look at. It *was* beautiful. Ethan's kid sister had gotten the Regis gym so perfectly she must have visited just to do the drawing. It was in the same style as the Screech Neck picture, black ink and some kind of paint or wet marker for the colors. One of our players was making a basket and everyone was cheering. I remember being particularly impressed with how well she had done the shooter's hands. Hands are tough.

"Nice," I said, hoping they would both read some deadly

sarcasm into my one-word critique. Then I spun and headed out of the alley. Landon was waiting at the edge of the seats, and I led him up to the back, where we sat with the others. The bleachers creaked a bit from Landon's weight, enough to make Erica look up from her spiral bondage. I used the opportunity to hand her one of the popcorn bags.

Before taking it, she looked at Landon and said, "*The Rule* makes strange bedfellows, eh?"

"Got that right," I said as Ethan and Vicky clambered up to join us. Vicky sat next to me and patted me on the leg. Ethan sat stiff-backed next to her and pretended to be looking at the rest of the gym. Occasionally, he whistled to himself. Erica gave them a wide-eyed look. I think she was pleased.

"Going to offer me some popcorn?" Vicky asked me with a campaign-button grin.

"I'm thinking no," I said. I was afraid she was going to ask why, but she didn't—and we got down to the serious business of watching the most stunningly lame game in the history of basketball.

No, really. After the first five minutes, it made me want to put on vampire contact lenses and wear black lipstick. The Hurricanes were practically unconscious, dropping the ball, tripping over it, missing easy layups, screwing up like crazy. On our side, it was nice to see that Mike was actually a decent player. He even made a few good shots, but despite all that, for the entire game, Regis stayed ahead by at least two points.

As the clock ticked away the remaining minutes of the fourth quarter with us still losing, Dylan, Landon, and Vicky looked stricken, deeply worried, horribly nervous. Erica would look up occasionally, then go back to her writing as if nothing important ever happened in the real world. Grace, bless her, never lost her grin, and Ethan? He just kept watching. Never moved his head, and he had that smug little smile on his face, like he knew the miracle was going to happen, and it didn't matter what he was seeing.

He spotted me watching him, grinned, then chanted softly, "The Screech Neck Basket Cases will win this game. The Screech Neck Basket Cases will win this game."

Landon started chanting, too. "The Screech Neck Basket Cases will win this game."

Vicky joined in. "The Screech Neck Basket Cases will win this game."

She nudged Erica, who looked up as if she'd been asleep. "What? Oh yes. The Screech Neck Basket Cases will win this game."

I'd just popped a big handful of golden, delicious popcorn in my mouth when they all nodded at me to join in. "The Screech Neck Basket Cases will win this game. The Screech Neck Basket Cases will win this game."

So, still chewing, I did. "The Screech Neck Basket Cases will . . . ack!"

A whole kernel, probably the only one in the bunch that didn't pop, had, as Joey likes to say, "gone down the wrong hole."

I started hacking. "Ackk . . . ackk."

The others kept chanting. "The Screech Neck Basket Cases will win this game."

My coughing got so loud, a few players looked up at me from the court. Fortunately, they were Regis players, and their distraction let Mike dribble through and make a shot. The score was now 31–29 in favor of Regis.

Erica leaned over and thwacked me on the back. The kernel flew out, and I could chant again: "The Screech Neck Basket Cases will win this game."

The few kids there from our school, people who weren't even members of the Crave, joined in: "The Screech Neck Basket Cases will win this game."

Now Mike had the ball and was driving it madly down the court. Now half the tiny crowd was chanting:

"The Screech Neck Basket Cases will win this game."

One basket could tie it, then there'd be overtime. If that didn't happen, it'd be over. Instead of picturing my spork and chanting, I clenched my hands and shouted, "Come on! Come on!"

The Regis defense was coming up fast on Mike's side, but he faked them out and drove for the net. The ball flew . . .

"The Screech Neck Basket Cases will win this game."

. . . and hit the rim.

It bounced straight into the waiting hands of a Regis player, who dribbled it back to the midcourt nice and slow, taking his time, running out the clock. With five seconds left and our boys bearing down on him, he passed it to someone else. Four seconds. It was passed again . . . only this time, Mike snagged it out of midair.

As the clock hit two seconds, he was at the wrong end of the court. For the first second, he looked totally lost.

This time, I joined in. "The Screech Neck Basket Cases will . . ."

"Shoot!" his coach and half the audience screamed.

He did. Up and away. The buzzer sounded with the ball in midair. From where we sat, it looked like the shot was way off, like it wouldn't even reach the backboard.

It didn't.

But it did hit the net when it went through. A three-pointer!

Like the people said, the Screech Neck Basket Cases had won the game, 33–32!

Dylan, Erica, Landon, Grace, Vicky, and Ethan flew up out of their seats, cheering. I leaped in the air and nearly fell off the back of the bleachers. Even some of the Regis kids cheered our guys.

I landed just in time to see Vicky gave Ethan a big hug. Oh, it looked enough like a friendly hug, but I found myself not leaping up and down so much anymore.

I stood there overwhelmed, feeling like I'd won something, feeling like I'd lost something more. I must have stayed that way a long time, because people began filing past me. Ethan patted me on the shoulder on his way out. So did Vicky, after she flashed me a grin. Landon wasn't the touchy-feely type, but I could see he was smiling, too.

Only Erica stopped and gave me a hug. It wasn't a congratulatory kind of hug. More of an I'm-so-sorry-for-your-loss kind of thing.

She whispered in my ear, "Maybe we can get together and imanifest a car accident for Ethan."

Erica, always with the death images. This one, though, I kind of liked.

I guess she could tell I didn't feel like talking, because she went on ahead with the rest of the crowd. Soon, I was alone in the gym, taking in the empty space, not really knowing what to feel.

Realizing I wasn't going to decide anytime soon, and realizing I still had to drive everyone home, I turned to leave, but before I did, I glanced back at the seats. I was still imagining Ethan and Vicky hugging, I guess, but I noticed something else. Erica's book.

It was totally bizarre that she had left it there. For Erica, it was kind of like leaving your head behind. I nabbed it.

And yeah, of course I looked at it. I was secretly worried she'd left it behind on purpose for me to find, and there'd be some sort of note for me. Not an I-love-you note, more of a how-dare-you-look-at-my-journal note.

But I flipped through it anyway. Y'ever see that horror movie *The Shining*, where Jack Nicholson's wife finds the novel he's supposedly writing, and it's just the same thing written over and over again about how all work and no play made him a dull boy, and this proved, in a really creepy way, that he was totally psycho?

Well, there it was, right in front of me, page after page after page after page, the same thing over and over again, in Erica's small but immaculate handwriting:

> I will pass my next algebra test.
> I will pass my next algebra test.
> I will pass my next algebra test.
> I will pass my next algebra test.

I mean, it filled the *entire* book.

- I would still like the greatest gaming system in the world, the Xbox. A 733 MHz Intel main processor and 233 MHz graphics processor from nVidia create photorealistic graphics in real time. A huge hard drive stores saved games and characters, and a built-in Ethernet port enables super-fast multiplayer online gaming over a broadband Internet connection. —Landon

- My brother Dave is overseas. He taught me everything I know about skateboarding. He can do a terrific ollie. Lately, they've been sending him to some hot spots. We IM each other once a week when he's at base. I have to get up at 3 A.M. to do it, but we were always really close. A friend of his got killed by an IED last week. When I tried to talk to Dave about it, he got all weird. So, screw the skateboard move, if this book actually works, what I really want most is to have him back home safe and sound, job done. —Alex

- Shoes, check, tank top, check, but really, I've been feeling a little selfish lately, so now I'm thinking I should be worried a little more about all the problems in the world. I think we should work on world hunger or world peace or global warming or world something. —Beth

- So is *The Rule of Won*, like, a miracle or what? School funding! Basketball winners! I was so excited about the game, I ordered this custom version of the "1" pin made of gold with some real diamond dust in it. It took all my allowance for a few months, but I'm not worried about that! The universe is one of eternal abundance! I don't even know what to want next! —Grace

- I have a friend hooked on crystal meth. He's in the hospital now, and they say he might have some brain damage. I want him to be okay. —Jacob

- *The Rule* rocks! My boyfriend and I are back together and I was made weekend manager at Barry's Books! Everyone says my outlook has improved and I'm smiling all the time. Okay, so I haven't gotten the little red Porsche I've been trying to imanifest, but I know it's just a matter of time. —Colleen

- I will pass my next algebra test. I will pass my next algebra test. I will pass my next algebra test. I will pass my next algebra test. I will pass my next algebra test. I will pass my next algebra test. I will pass my next algebra test. I will pass my next algebra test.

I will pass my next algebra test. I will pass my next algebra test. I will pass my next algebra test. I will pass my next algebra test. —Erica

- I couldn't believe it. I heard some kids in the hall razzing *The Rule*, like it was something they knew anything about. It got me so furious, I slammed my books against the wall they were leaning against, and they scattered fast. I'm not supposed to make fun of people's beliefs, right? So why should I put up with it when someone makes fun of mine? —Dylan

- Yeah, Basket Cases! And thank you all for my last shot! I know it's probably not a big deal to anybody else, and I'm fine if someone else comes up with something that can help everyone, but I could really use a raise at McD's. I need some repairs on my car. It's got like 215k miles on it, but I think I could get it running for a couple hundred bucks. —Mike

- I'd really just like to be able to move on with my life, forget the past, and focus on the future, whatever it may be. —Caleb

- The election is in four days! I'm up for whatever, but I just hope everyone remembers to vote—and to remember me when they do! I'm sure I can do a lot of good for the school and for our Crave! —Vicky

- The whole basketball thing has me weirded. I mean, did we give those guys the flu? I'm going to take a break to try and think some of this through. Doesn't look like you'll miss me much, what with all the new members. —Dana

- That stomach flu was amazing! Nicole got it and was out for a week! Her damn iPhone is still chugging along, but I think I'm getting closer. —Sophia

- My party was totally absolutely terrifically amazing! I managed to clean up before my folks got home and even replaced what we took from their liquor cabinet. So my Crave this time is for another get-together soon! Lock and load! Hey, did we win the game? —Jane

- I really want to thank everyone for saying hello to me whenever they see me; it really lifts my spirits! After being so unpopular for so long, I am so happy to have a bunch of new friends, and I'm thrilled about the basketball team, too! —Olivia

- I just want to say that whatever the group decides, I hope we're careful in a way to phrase it so that no one else gets hurt, like with the flu, even if they do wish it upon themselves. Patience and peace for everyone! —Will

- So I got that date with that girl and it was going absolutely fantastic until the very end, when I guess I was so busy thinking this was a dream come true and I could finally have whatever I wanted, that I misread her signals. She got pretty upset and told her parents. I'd really like that part to just go away. —Jeff

- You guys should be careful what you wish for. Now that I have the guy I thought was the love of my life, frankly he's turned into kind of a pain, following me all over the place, IMing me constantly, embarrassing me in front of my friends. I still like him, I guess, but I really want some time to myself. Do you think maybe we could all work on making him back off a little? —Kathleen

- Can you freaking believe it? My mother gets the freaking raise, but instead of taking some freaking time off like she said, so I could have some time off from babysitting, she all of a sudden freaking announces she wants to use the money to go back to college, which means more babysitting time for me! Really, after I spent all that time chanting for her, I deserve better. That money's really mine, in a way. —Hailey

- Better cafeteria food! This slop makes me sick! —Benjamin

- I'd just like everyone to be really honest with themselves and take a good look at what's going on around us. I think it's great that we're doing all this good stuff, and how much the club is growing, but I don't think we need a special salute in the hallways. —Anonymous

- I really want people to stop thinking I'm gay. There's nothing wrong with it, but I'm not, you know? Just because I like art and Broadway shows does *not* make me gay. That is such a stupid stereotype. —Andrew

- I still have the dreams. I don't think the meds are working, and the guy in the lunchroom saw me looking at him and now he keeps staring at me, like he knows I'm thinking he's a killer. Now I'm worried that maybe the dream is trying to warn me about him, and that maybe I should carry a knife to school to protect myself. But I could never get it past the metal detectors. Could I? —Lauren

It can be tough work being a slacker. Yeah, that sounds ridiculous, but really, there are times when it takes more effort not to do something than to do it. Like, over the next few days, I really had to fight with myself not to grab Vicky and demand that she tell me what was going on with her and Ethan. I also had to stop myself from demanding that Erica do some actual studying, because she was totally freaking me out.

Doing either seemed like a bad idea, though. I pretty much knew what was going on with Vicky and Ethan. And Erica? Aside from the fact that it was ridiculous for someone like me to tell *anyone* to study, how could I even suggest *The Rule* might not always totally work? Wasn't I just being a wussy doubter anyway? Hadn't we all just seen it, big-time, twice?

Anyone who hadn't seen it sure heard about it. Ethan, Vicky, Grace, Landon, Dylan, and the others made sure of that—hanging posters all over the place, bragging about our successes. As a result, the Crave was getting so big it made me nervous, especially since some of the posts on the board were getting creepier than Erica's notebook.

I mean, the funding was just kind of fun to think about, and the basketball game was, well, a *game*, but Erica was messing with her future, and the posts were getting serious and seriously weird. Like that twitchy girl Lauren, who was thinking of bringing a knife to school. I tried to talk to her about that, but every time I got near her, she just huddled up and walked away, like I was a serial killer waiting to happen.

So there I was, Super-slacker, struggling not to act. At times the only thing stopping me was a firmly held belief that there was nothing I *could* do other than think of my spork and chant, "Everything's gonna be just fine. Everything's gonna be just fine."

Instead of easing my mind, the construction only added to my newfound spiritual anxiety. Everywhere I went, classroom to cafeteria, I heard popping nail guns and whining drills, the singsong of our fallen gym wing rising from the grave:

Pht! Pht! Zzz! Zzz!

Every day by midday, I had one freaking big headache.

Did I mention Vicky won the election? Surprise, surprise. And ever since, Madame President didn't have any free time—not for me, anyway. I noticed something else about her that just made me sad. I don't know if it was because she was president now or because she was worried about what Ethan thought, but she clipped her nails and stopped painting little pictures on them.

At least I didn't vote for her.

(To be honest, by the time I remembered there was a vote, it was over.)

It was all getting to be too much. But like it or not, life goes on, or went on, or slouches on, until one day, as I walked toward bio, desperately trying to imanifest some aspirin for myself, a new sound wheedled its way above all the *pht!* and *zzz!* A sound that would change things, for me at least: the sound of paper being yanked off the wall.

Rip, rip, rip.

Mr. Eldridge, our "tough" math teacher, was tearing down Crave posters, one after the other.

Frankly, it seemed . . . *unholy*.

Kind of stunned, I walked up and stood at his back. I was so close that if I'd stretched, I could have touched my chin to the top of his shiny dome head. Not that I'd want to.

Rip, rip, rip.

"Mr. Eldridge?" I said. "Whatcha doin?"

He nearly leaped out of his skin.

In tried-and-true *Rule* believer mode, I got all offended and annoyed. I stared at him, like, "Well, young man? Do you have an explanation for this?"

Usually he has this calm look, like he's heard it all and nothing some student could ever say would faze or interest him, but now his face looked a little red, maybe from embarrassment, like he thought he was secretly invisible, and no one was supposed to notice he was tearing down posters.

"I . . . ," he finally said, clearing his throat. "I just don't think it's right for some club to take credit for our team's hard work or our new grant. You kids have enough trouble making it out there without putting your faith in crap like this."

Eldridge wasn't the sort to fail me in trig just because I stood up for myself, so I tapped the pin on my collar. "I don't think it's crap. Thirty million people don't think it's crap."

"Unbelievable," he said, more to himself than to me. "Science teachers can't mention God *or* teach evolution without an uproar, but something this patently absurd slips in right under the radar and no one blinks. Perfect for someone like you, eh, Dunne? Everything supposedly comes to you without you having to lift a finger."

Now he wasn't just attacking *The Rule*, he was after my slacker ways. The little adrenaline rush was just what I needed to clear my head. All of a sudden, I was totally sure about everything.

"I'm passing trig without lifting a finger, aren't I, Mr. E?"

"Yes. So far. You're facile, Dunne, that's clear. But don't confuse being facile with being smart. Things come easily to you so you're not used to working for them."

"Is it smart to be afraid of new ideas?" I said, nodding at the papers in his hand.

I thought I got him with that, but he just smiled. "You think *The Rule of Won* is a new idea?"

Fortunately, I'd read the book and even remembered some of it. "Well, technically, no. Knowledge of *The Rule* is ancient, but it was concealed for centuries, to keep people down, to oppress people."

"Dunne, the only reason anyone needs to oppress people

is to get something they want or to keep something they have: security, control over limited resources, wealth. If, like your *Rule* insists, everyone can have whatever they want whenever they want it just by asking, what's the point in keeping it secret?"

Ha. I had an answer. I said, "Uh . . ."

He crossed his arms. "Let's say that part's just an advertising gimmick, okay? Your book also says we get *only* what we ask for. Every rape victim the world over, every victim of child abuse, of war, of famine, of disease, deep down really asked for it. It's all the victim's fault."

He spoke with a kind of certainty Ethan could only imitate. Not droning or suave, like he was trying to hypnotize, but pleading and sincere, like he really wanted me to realize there was this tiger behind me that I just didn't see, and if I didn't move out of the way, it was going to get me.

I felt his words push at me like physical things, but I managed to hold my ground. After all, this was stuff I'd been thinking about for weeks. "How do you know life *doesn't* work that way? Isn't it possible people's expectations are always screwing them up?"

"Sure, sometimes, but your book says it's *always* true. What about a baby who dies in a car accident? A baby, who doesn't even know it's *in* a car. Where's the baby's expectations?"

I guess the look on my face told him I didn't have an immediate answer for that one either.

"Think about it, Dunne; you're not stupid. The *real* secret of life has got to be a lot more interesting and beautiful than a world that gives you whatever garbage you feel like asking for, doesn't it?"

Still offended, but now a little confused, I grabbed at the one thing I knew he couldn't argue with, not really. I pointed at the scrunched poster in his hand. "Even if you're right, Mr. E, don't you think people should be allowed to make up their own minds about it? See for themselves whether it works or not?"

He looked at me, looked at the posters in his hand, and made a hissing sound, like all the air had been let out of his head. Then he stormed off, leaving me alone with the sounds of power tools mixing with his arguments in my head.

It felt just like when the basketball game was over. I'd won the argument, but also, I'd lost.

I mean, what *about* that baby? What about Erica?

Still grumpy a short while later, I spotted Alden Moore and his crack reporting squad. They were exiting their precious newspaper office, all four laden with boxes.

The newspaper, and the article vindicating me, had yet to appear, so all in all I wasn't feeling too great about them. All talk. At least as a true slacker, I never promise to do anything in the first place.

I was going to ask about my article when I realized they were moving out.

"They move you because of the construction?"

Moore shot me an icy look. "No."

"So, what? You're redecorating? Really, if you spent half

the time actually putting out the paper that you do *talking* about it . . ."

Mason puckered her features into a pointy, antagonistic shape and said, "We're being kicked out. Another club, a much more *important* club, is taking our space."

"Which club?" By the time I asked the question, I realized I already knew the answer.

"Ask your girlfriend, Vicky," Drik said with unusual venom.

"She's not . . . I mean, what do you mean?"

Moore, struggling with his boxes, leaned against the wall. "*El presidente* apparently pulled some strings so your Crazy Cravers got our space."

"You're kidding!"

This, of course, was square-man Guy's opportunity to practice sarcasm. "Yeah, we're kidding. We're packing everything up just to have a laugh with you."

"We think someone in the Crave found out about the exposé we planned, so they moved against us," Moore said.

Guy eyed me suspiciously. "*You* knew we were planning that article, didn't you, Dunne?"

"Oh sure, my fault the building comes down. My fault you lose your office. My fault when it rains. Blame the slacker. You think maybe the fact that *The Ottis* or whatever hasn't come out with one issue yet might have something to do with it?"

"*The Otus*! We've had some problems!" Mason burst out. Her voice was so high pitched and defensive, I had to take a step back.

"Geez, take a breath. It's not that bad, is it? You still have an office, right?"

"For now, but we get to keep it only if we find a new adviser," Moore said. "We lost our old one same day as the space."

Mason reached out and patted his shoulder. "And Alden's allergic to mold."

"What happened to the adviser?"

"Mr. Giddich. Wyatt's brother-in-law. Wanted us to just print notices about meetings and letters from the administration. Any time we suggested anything that might ruffle feathers, he nixed it. That's why the paper hasn't come out. We finally confronted him about it last week. He said if we were really serious, we'd be better off with someone else."

Moore moved forward. "So, if you don't mind, I'd like to get this stuff into our new digs before my asthma meds wear off . . ."

He shifted his boxes, about to leave.

I was about to let him, when I saw Erica skirting the wall, writing in her book, an intense, grim look on her face as her hand scratched across the page. I shuddered to think what she was writing.

And again, I started to think about that baby.

"Wait," I said to Moore. "You can ask Eldridge to advise you. I bet he'll say yes."

"The math teacher?"

"Yeah. Tell him about that article you want to do on the Crave. Tell him . . . tell him I sent you."

Moore nodded. He and his well-oiled fighting machine marched off.

Once they were out of sight, I felt sick. I had to steady myself against the wall, my heart racing. What had I done? Eldridge. I had told them about Eldridge. I not only did something, but I did something and I didn't know why. Wasn't I still part of the Crave? Didn't I believe in *The Rule*?

My brain was bubbling the rest of the morning, feelings bouncing around my innards like the rubber balls in a handball court. I had not only betrayed the Crave, but my strongest slacker instincts had weakened and something else, something alien to me, was gaining strength.

When lunchtime came around, I saw Ethan and Vicky sitting together. In another uncharacteristic move, I decided I had to talk to them. Hard as it was, I was hoping Ethan could set me straight, say a few words that would blow the doubts away.

As I walked closer, I realized that though their spot was cozy, it wasn't so quiet. The construction crews sounded like they were just on the other side of the wall, and the noise of their tools grew louder with each step.

Pht! Pht! Zzz! Zzz!

I was surprised they heard me approach, but Vicky and Ethan looked up, unembarrassed. I didn't even say hi to Vicky. What I did say was, "Ethan, some of the stuff that's going on is getting me worried."

He pulled himself away from Vicky a bit, straightened his back so his blue shirt looked like a smooth second skin, and looked me in the eye. "Such as?"

Pht! Pht! Zzz! Zzz!

"Some of the Craves are so serious," I told him. "Like that guy who wants his brother home from the war."

He shrugged with one shoulder, like my doubts weren't worth both. "Are you saying they shouldn't try to imanifest the best possible things for the people they love?"

"No . . . I guess I'm saying, what if it doesn't work? What if they don't do something else that might work because they're busy with this? They'll be hurt."

Pht! Pht! Zzz! Zzz!

"Why wouldn't it work?" Ethan said.

Vicky spoke up. "You've already seen what we can do. Why shouldn't we take our lives seriously and try for more important things? It's a natural next step."

Ethan nodded as if it were as obvious as the table they were sitting at.

"What about Lauren wanting to bring a knife to school to protect herself?"

"Oh. I can see why *that* might worry you, but remember, she has to follow her own path. She has to work these things through herself."

"What if she works them through with a knife?"

"That won't happen," Ethan said. "As long as we watch our negative thoughts."

Pht! Pht! Zzz! Zzz!

"How can you be sure?"

Vicky was about to speak again, but Ethan stopped her. "The same way we can be sure about everything. The same way we *have* to be sure about everything. You just need to believe in yourself more. That's how it works. Certainty. Project a positive reality, and reality will respond. It's *The Rule*."

Whatever this new thing in me was, it was really starting to get pissed off.

"I believe in me, fine," I snapped. "It's other people I worry about. Like Erica."

"Erica? What about her?"

In frustration, my hands flew up in the air. "She was always a little dark, but now she's doing this freaky scene from *The Shining*, writing the same thing over and over again about how she's going to pass algebra."

Ethan smiled. "Good for her. If she does it sincerely, she'll pass."

"Even without studying?"

Ethan nodded. "She's in the class, isn't she? She's hearing everything the teacher says, and her brain is recording it. It's just buried in her subconscious. Imanifesting that passing grade *is* studying, only not small-time with calculations and textbooks, but big-time, with the *real* goal in mind. Taking full advantage of her mind."

Vicky nodded. They seemed so damn sure of themselves.

Why not? There was the grant and the basketball game, and the constant, hammering noise that was giving me a headache.

Pht! Pht! Zzz! Zzz!

Wasn't that the sound of *The Rule*'s success?

Vicky spoke again. "Why don't you trust it?"

Pht! Pht! Zzz! Zzz!

"I just . . . I'm just worried. What if they don't do it right, what if they fail?"

"Stop thinking that way. Thinking that way is hurting them," Ethan said.

Vicky reached out and took my hands. "Don't worry. Ethan and I are imanifesting together so that no harm will come to anyone."

Pht! Pht! Zzz! Zzz!

"So that no harm comes to anyone? You putting force fields around them? What are you guys, like, superheroes now, or gods?"

My voice was getting louder with every word, but Ethan kept his low and steady.

"We're all gods, more or less," he said.

As I spun and left, his voice echoed in my head, punctuated by a constant rush of *Pht! Pht! Zzz! Zzz!*

As soon as I was sure they couldn't see me anymore, I clamped my hands to my ears and ran. I didn't stop until I was outside, on the far side of the school, so far away that the sounds of the construction were distant and muffled.

I'd really, really been hoping Ethan would stop my doubts. Instead, he was just starting to look really, really nuts.

Dr. Wyatt was strutting around birdlike with the construction workers. He didn't even stop to point at me or ask why I wasn't in school.

I was no longer a consideration. Invisible.

Something I'd always wanted. Which reminded me of

something else Joey likes to say, something that girl mentioned on the board: "Be careful what you wish for, you might get it."

Pretty funny in the context of *The Rule*, eh?

During my last period, I sat near the door and snuck out a few minutes early to head to the trailers. Our Crave would be meeting to pick our next goal. I needed badly to know what the hell I was doing, and I didn't anymore, so I wanted to get there early, catch Ethan alone. I wanted to have him talk some sense into me, or try to talk some sense into him. I thought things might be a little clearer in my head if Vicky weren't right there with him.

But of course, no such luck.

They were already together in the trailer, packing up two small boxes. When she saw me, Vicky gave me a button smile. I kind of froze.

"Hi, Caleb," she said. Maybe she was worried after lunch I might not show at all, and now she thought I was *accepting* things. "I wanted it to be a surprise, but this will be our last meeting here. We've got the old newspaper office."

"Yeah, I heard."

"Oh. Well, we're just going to run some stuff over there for next week. Be right back."

She picked up one box and walked toward me. When I didn't move right away, she looked over her shoulder. "Come on, Ethan."

He hadn't stopped gaping at me since I'd come to the doorway. Maybe after lunch he was hoping I *wouldn't* show. Vicky's voice pulled him out of his trance.

"Right."

He grabbed the second box, then gave his backpack, which was sitting on a chair, a nervous glance. Pretending I hadn't noticed, I stepped out of Vicky's way.

"Come on, Ethan," Vicky said. "Don't want the Crave to start late."

"Right," he said again, and followed her out.

There we were, me, the mold, and Ethan's bag. The last bell would ring any second, and the Cravers would show. I could've just waited, or left. Instead I stepped over to the bag and noticed a rolled-up sheet of drawing paper packed carefully to the side. I figured it was his sister's drawing of the basketball game, until I pulled off the rubber band and unrolled it.

It was his sister's all right, and man, was she a terrific artist. Only it wasn't the basketball game, or the school. It was a picture of our cafeteria serving great, delicious new food. No sporks either, but real knives and forks. The roast ham with pineapple slices looked so real, you could taste it.

It was obviously the next Crave Ethan had chosen. I thought it was kind of arrogant for him to tell his sister about it before the rest of us, but then again, why should his arrogance surprise me?

Hearing the bell, I rerolled the picture, snapped the rubber band back on, and shoved the drawing back in his bag. I should have felt guilty, but I didn't. There was something really strange about how . . . how *orchestrated* this all felt.

People filed in. Lots. At least half I'd never seen before. Nodding to those I knew, I sat down way in the back. Good thing, too, because we quickly ran out of chairs. By the time Erica showed, nose in book, it was standing room only. Barely noticing me or anything else, she wedged her way past some people and leaned against the far wall.

"Hey," I called to her. "Want my seat?"

My voice muffled by the bodies, I had to say it again, louder.

I was hoping for some dark and deathly quote, but she didn't say a word. She looked up from her writing just long enough to shake her head.

"Erica," I called.

She looked up again. "Yes?"

I studied her face. She looked even more intense than usual and, if possible, more pale. Her eyes had circles under them and she was wearing thick makeup, like she was trying to hide how tired she was but was too tired to make it work. For days I'd wanted to talk to her about what I'd found in her notebook, but had no idea what to say.

"Good luck with your studying," I called out.

The right side of her lip rose in a wry Mona Lisa smile, making her look a little more like the Erica I knew, or at least imagined I knew. I was thinking of bagging my chair and standing next to her, but Ethan and Vicky picked that moment to return, both wide-eyed at how big our Crave had grown.

Vicky mouthed "Wow!" at me, then stood off to the side near the front of the room. Ethan, grinning ear to ear, did his teacher thing. He welcomed everyone, especially the newcomers. Once the whoops and hollers trailed off, he again rattled off the basics, for those of us, as they say on TV, joining the show in progress.

At this stage of things I wasn't sure whether I believed in this stuff at all anymore, but I desperately wanted something to decide for me, something to make it all work, something that made sense.

"Okay, if everyone's clear on all that, why don't we move on to our next Crave? This week I've picked . . ."

My hand shot up.

"Ethan?"

He didn't even look at me, as if he were pretending I wasn't there.

"Hey, Ethan? Ethan?"

Finally, his head snapped toward me. "Yeah?"

"Why don't we put this one up for a vote?" I said.

Something unusual happened next. Perfectly poised Ethan shook his head in a kind of anxious, twitchy way. For the first time that I'd heard, he hesitated when he spoke.

"I . . . don't know if we're ready for that," he said.

"Why not?" I asked, looking around. "We've been through two big Craves together already."

As Ethan took a few seconds to compose his answer, the crowd murmured. I glanced at Vicky long enough to see her angry stare, which I found oddly satisfying.

Ethan was about ready to speak again, but before he could, the now Goth-less Landon, still wearing that too-small hoodie, put in his two cents.

"That wouldn't work. Everyone would just vote for their own Crave," he said.

I shrugged. "I won't," I said. "I'll vote for Erica's."

At the sound of her name, Erica picked up her head and looked around nervously.

I continued. "Come on. We got funding for the school, the Basket Cases won—how hard can an algebra test be?"

I was quite tickled I'd thought of it. Mr. E was right, I am facile. If it worked, it solved all my worries. I could continue to believe in the book, even if I didn't particularly like Ethan, and I wouldn't have to worry that Erica was headed for a loony bin. And if it didn't work . . .

Mike stuck his hand up. "Hey, why don't we imanifest *everyone* in the class passing that algebra exam? It'd help out the school, maybe even raise our standing in the state."

Good old Mike. Now people were nodding. They liked the idea, regardless of what Ethan's sister had drawn.

"I . . . ?" Ethan said.

He was looking around, hoping someone else would talk, but they were all waiting to hear from him.

After letting him sweat a second, I said cheerfully, "Why don't we at least vote on whether we should vote?"

Now *everyone*, everyone except Ethan and Vicky, was nodding.

Ethan scanned us, weighing the mood of the crowd. That mad scientist look flashed in his eyes again, only not the kind you get when you've just created life from the dead, the kind you get when the monster you've created is about to hurl you off the top of the castle.

"Uh . . . fine," he said.

You ever see a high school student put up a hand and say, "Nah, I really don't think I should be trusted with a decision"? Of course everyone voted to be allowed to vote.

After that, I stayed quiet while Ethan made a little speech in favor of better food in the cafeteria. But hey, once Mike talked about a whole class passing an algebra test, Ethan's choice seemed downright petty. Even Ethan knew it; you could tell by how his voice trailed off more and more, how he winced when he mentioned the value of good nutrition.

So in the end, Vicky won one election, and I felt like I'd won one, too.

Ethan led us all in a meditation to conjure a mesmory. From the black infinity of my iceberg mind, my faithful spork rose in a snap, and soon we were chanting, in unison, "Everyone will pass the algebra test. Everyone will pass the algebra test."

I caught Erica trying to keep herself from smiling too widely. There was even some color to her cheeks. Maybe she was blushing? I hoped I hadn't embarrassed her too much.

After the meeting, I was pleased to see Ethan looking shaken. Hey, it was probably because the group had grown so large so fast, and, you know, the air was pretty close in that trailer. Or not.

Vicky went up to him and they whispered to each other. I didn't hang around to listen. I did look back through the open door a few times as I moved across the parking lot. First, I saw them standing there together. I looked back again a few seconds later, but they'd vanished inside, probably to finish packing the place up, or to curse my name.

I was just nearing the bus stop when a hand made its way to my shoulder.

"Thank you so much," a surprisingly gentle voice said.

It was Erica. For once, she wasn't writing in her book.

"I . . . ," she said, flailing her fingers in front of her as if trying to shake out the words. "Just . . . thanks."

"You're welcome," I said. We walked quietly toward the bus. When we stopped, I looked at her again.

"Do me a little favor, Erica?"

"Your wish is my command."

"Could you at least study, *too?*"

Her face twisted, but her brow frowned. Her lips smiled, but her eyes looked pensive. This was one complicated girl.

"Okay," she finally said. "Okay."

Near as I could tell, after that, Vicky wasn't talking to me anymore.

By that, I mean I'd say, "Hey, Vicky!" to her really loudly and even though it was completely obvious she'd heard me, she'd keep walking.

On the other hand, the rest of the Crave couldn't get enough of me. I was getting all these "Hey, Calebs!" and pats on the back—sometimes from people I didn't even know, which, frankly, can be a little unsettling. I felt like a hypocrite, especially since Eldridge was now the school newspaper's adviser and my own faith in *The Rule* wasn't exactly steadfast. But having gotten that vote thing going, it was like I'd established myself as a kind of second leader. I don't think anyone disliked Ethan, I think people just like to see authority challenged, and, well, Ethan had set himself up for that.

Meanwhile, the group tripled in size. You could see those little "1" pins everywhere now. The Cravers had even taken to imanifesting in the hallways, which had its own dark strangeness. More often than not, it wasn't enough to just say hi when you saw a fellow Craver. No, you had to look each other in the eyes, grin, and say together, "Everyone will pass the algebra test!"

Aside from being cheesy, it got old fast.

Worse, some kids looked like they were afraid *not* to chant, especially when Dylan or one of his pals was around. He'd gotten a couple of other jocks to join up, and they were all acting kind of like the Gestapo. I was disappointed to see Mike hanging with them. Thought he was better than that. So now, we had, like, a secret police, which I don't recall reading about anywhere in the book.

If any of them saw you skip a chant, they'd get up in your face and practically scream, "Come on! Everyone will pass the algebra test! Everyone will pass the algebra test!"

I found myself being forced to chant, a lot. But if it worked, what the hell?

Erica and I were chatting all the time now, on the bus, in the halls, in class. She even called me once or twice just to gab. Turns out her folks were professors at some university, which I guess explains her literary bent. Neither knew a lick of math, which I guess explains her algebra problems. Her mom was fired because of politics, whatever that means, and her dad quit in disgust. Now they're in PR at a friend's business about an hour away from Screech Neck, barely making ends meet. The scholarship she'd mentioned on the board? It was the only way she could afford college.

Which explained her desperation.

And made me worry about her more. As a friend. I think. A really good friend, anyway.

I wasn't sure just how much studying she was doing, but the circles under her eyes had disappeared and her mood lightened a bit, which in the case of Erica Black was the same as saying the sun was shining at night.

"Hey, you magnificent slouching beast!" she cheerfully called one Screech Neck morning a few days after our last Crave.

"Hey?" I said, not sure she was talking to me. That was one thing I liked about her—she was definitely the kind of girl who made you think.

She came closer, books held against her chest the way girls carry them sometimes. "Yes, Mr. Dunne, it's you I'm greeting, you, wonderful you, glorious you."

She stopped about a foot from me and I noticed she had this smile on her face. It was odd to see her smile sincerely in the first place, but this one quivered a bit, almost like she was bursting with good feeling.

"Thanks," I answered. "Is it the clothes?"

I stuck my arms out, vaguely modeling my standard oil-stained overshirt. The T-shirt I wore beneath it had the poster from the movie *Slacker* on it. A classic everyone should run out and rent.

"Hmm . . . I think it's more your . . . your . . . *je ne sais quoi*."

I knew what that meant. I'm not dumb, just lazy. It was French for "I don't know what"—a certain something that can't be put into words. Only for some reason I didn't remember that at the time, so I just nodded and said, "Ah."

Then out of nowhere she said, "Want to get together after school and study algebra with me?"

"Oh. Me? Study?"

"Yes. It involves books. They have many pages and contain a lot of information. People sometimes read them for knowledge and pleasure."

"I knew that," I said. "It's just . . ."

All of a sudden I started thinking that maybe Erica and I had been talking a little *too* much. Did she think I'd championed her Crave because I, you know, had secret feelings for her? I felt closer to her, but with everything else going on, I didn't know if I wanted to head anywhere with that.

I wanted to say something to let her know where I was at, but I didn't want whatever I said to send her rushing back to the dark planet she called home. So I began the same way someone always does when they're about to say something awkward.

I frowned and said, "Look, Erica—"

"Oh," she said, reaching into her bag. "I baked you some cookies."

"Cookies?"

She pulled out a small baggie with these thick chocolate chip suckers wedged inside. You could see they were moist from the way they clung to the plastic.

I *love* big moist chocolate chip cookies.

She held out the bag. When I didn't take it right away, she shook it, like I was a frightened squirrel she was trying to attract. It worked.

I took the cookies, pulled open the bag, and popped some chocolatey heaven into my mouth. Oh, they were good.

"Look, Erica," I said again, my mouth full.

I guess my words were garbled, because she said, "Tomorrow after school would be perfect," and wandered off down the hall.

I was torn between running after her to straighten things out and standing there while I sucked the bits of semisweet chocolate goodness from the hollows of my molars.

Maybe studying with her wouldn't be so bad. I did like her.

And maybe there'd be more cookies.

The warning bell rang. It was a free period for me, but security didn't cotton to folks exercising personal freedom in the hallways, so I headed to the library, planning to find a quiet corner to further enjoy my treat in private.

The construction crews must have been on break, too, because the noises were gone, making things extraordinarily pleasant. I'd just found a lounge chair and was curled up in it, munching away and eyeing a graphic novel someone had left on a table, when I spotted the First Couple of SNH, Ethan and Vicky, strutting by.

They gave me a look, but I flashed them a big chocolatey smile like I didn't have a care in the world. Once they passed, I followed them from the corners of my eyes. They sat in a love seat a few yards away. Every now and then I'd look up to see what they were doing.

The library was so quiet that ten minutes later, when Ethan's cell phone vibrated, I heard the buzz. After glancing at the caller ID, he hightailed it out a side door, Vicky in tow.

Relatively sure they'd forgotten about me, I stood and crept to the door. It had one of those shatterproof windows in it, with the wire embedded in the glass, so I could see Vicky standing outside, biting one of her bland, pictureless fingernails. Ethan leaned against the wall, head hunched over, hand cupping his cell phone to his ear. The phone was last year's model, but a fancy-ass thing. The numbers glowed red, lighting the bottom of his face a little in the dim hallway, making him look a little devilish.

The side door to the library is usually locked. On the way out, one of them must have kicked down the doorstop, to leave it open a crack so they could get back in. That meant if I got a little closer, I'd "accidentally" hear what they were saying. So I did.

Getting as near as I dared, I leaned back against one of the painted cinder-block walls that made up the door frame and looked sideways at them through the door window as I chewed a cookie.

Ethan was obviously upset at whatever he was hearing.

"What do you mean? I thought you wanted to help," he hissed. He shook his head "no" a bunch of times, like whoever was on the other end of the line could see him.

"Alyssa . . . Alyssa . . . listen . . . Yeah, yeah, of course people should study, but this is a different kind of studying . . . They're in the class all the time, listening subconsciously and . . ."

I could guess from the way his face rattled with rage that kid sister Alyssa really wasn't particularly interested in hearing about different kinds of studying.

Vicky was at his shoulder, tapping him, saying, "Tell her . . ." and then something I couldn't make out, but Ethan kept waving her off. After some agitated back and forth, he looked ready to blow.

I was starting to like Alyssa, even though I'd never met her. Aside from her talent as an artist, apparently she had some integrity because, judging from the way the color drained from Ethan's face, she was sticking to her guns.

He should have tried a cookie.

"Alyssa. I'm . . . Fine. Fine. FINE!"

He snapped his phone shut and turned to Vicky. This put me in his line of sight, so I darted to the side where I couldn't see them anymore and hoped they couldn't see me.

I could still hear them, though.

"She's got this stupid idea that people should pass or fail tests on their own, without imanifesting. She doesn't see the big picture . . ."

"I know you're worried—"

"I'm not. I'm not worried at all. No negative thoughts. This is great. Perfect. It's making me finally realize we don't need Alyssa's help. We never did. We have the power without her."

Hearing that, all the misgivings I'd been having about the Crave, *The Rule of Won*, and Ethan began sticking to each other like soft sugary nuggets of dough, rolling themselves into one big yummy chocolate chip cookie of doubt. Despite what he was saying, suave, sophisticated Ethan looked like he *wasn't* sure we didn't need his kid sister.

What was up with that? I mean, Alyssa was a great artist

and all, but did he think she was magic? Was she linked to his mesmories? Did she remind him of his dead mother? This was the first crack in his armor I'd seen, and for me, it was a big one.

I was thinking Mr. E and I should have a chat about how the universe worked, or didn't, and maybe this time I'd listen. But I didn't have trig again until tomorrow. It could wait a day, I figured.

The bell rang. Social studies. The side door was closer, but I didn't want to risk being spotted, so I grabbed my bags and hustled out front with the crowd.

It didn't work. By the time I'd rounded the corner, I heard Vicky calling, "Caleb! Caleb!"

It wasn't because she was speaking to me again; it was because she was angry—furious, from the look of her. She raced up, blond brow knitted, eyes flaring. She all but leaped in front of me, cutting off my path to the exit.

"Hey, Vi—"

"I saw you by the door. You were eavesdropping."

"I was not! What sort of person do you think I am?"

She stared at me. Lying was too much of an effort.

"Well, okay, maybe a little."

The crowd, trying to exit, moved to either side of us, bumping as they passed. I wanted to get away from Vicky fast, but it was like we were caught in a little bubble in the middle of a river of people.

"That was a private phone call!"

I shrugged. "Then he should have had it in private instead

of in the middle of a hallway. I mean, what is it with some people on cell phones that makes them think the world vanishes just because they're on a call?"

"You had no right. It was none of your business. I don't want you telling anyone else in the Crave about it. Not if you still want to be a member."

That brought me up short. Vicky threatening to kick me out? Vicky? The one who insisted I join in the first place? I didn't even know people *could* be kicked out.

It pissed me off.

"Yeah, well, I'm thinking of quitting anyway."

I think that surprised me more than it did her. Still, she was the one who took half a step back. "But . . . it's been so good for you."

"Has it? I'm not so sure."

Disgust filled her face. "Are you so into doing nothing that even wishing is too much of an effort?"

"It's more than that. The whole thing's getting screwy and something bizarre is going on with Ethan and his sister, isn't it? He's not sure *The Rule* works without her. Maybe that means he's not sure it works at all."

She crossed her arms. "If you heard that, then you heard him say we don't need her. The power is ours. It always has been. You're just afraid of that, Caleb, afraid of your own power, afraid of everyone else's. I used to be like you, but I'm not anymore. It's a great big world out there full of treasures, and I'm going to grab every one I can!"

"Like Ethan?"

She stumbled for a second, then looked defiant. "Yes, like Ethan. We're together now. And you didn't even try to stop *that*, did you?"

"Maybe . . . maybe I didn't want to."

She moved her head back, like I'd hit her, but an Ethan-like sneer came across her face pretty quickly. "That's just an excuse. You're a coward."

"Really? Why is it when something happens that Ethan doesn't want, it's still because somehow he really wanted it? Isn't that totally screwed up? I wanted it to happen even though I didn't want it to happen? What the hell does that mean? And if you're not afraid of anything, why don't you even paint your fingernails anymore, huh?"

I was shouting by the end of that, and if I thought Vicky wasn't talking to me before, she *really* wasn't talking to me now. She didn't move out of my way; she just stood there glaring. But she let me go.

I wasn't actually thinking of quitting before I said it, but I warmed to the idea fast. With the new gym wing almost up, my life was practically back to normal. Even if the book was right, this might be just the opportunity I needed to return full-time to my old independent slacker ways.

There were, unfortunately, two problems with this line of thinking.

The first was the other Cravers, who, as I'd already mentioned, were starting to get a tad fascistic. The group was so big now that quitting it could leave me as much on the outs at SNH as I was when everyone thought I'd destroyed the school.

The second was Erica. I already thought I should tell her I didn't want to be her boyfriend, but how could I also say I was thinking of quitting the Crave? There was a good chance one or both might yank her out of her algebra groove.

This being Thursday, and the midterm being on Monday, I took the slacker way out and decided it was best to do nothing and wait. I was hoping I could run some of this by Mr. Eldridge, though.

As it was, an old saying that contradicts the basic precepts of *The Rule of Won* turned out to be true: the best-laid plans of mice and men oft go astray.

The next day, Friday, Eldridge was out and we had a lame substitute who let us "read quietly" in our seats. This sucked. Eldridge was never absent. Eldridge was never sick. He didn't get sick. He was, after all, an alien or a high-powered robot from the future.

I was so disappointed not to have someone to bounce all these thoughts off of that I even considered speaking with Moore and Co., but I couldn't find them either. Mrs. D was available, but I was afraid she'd just tell me to float.

By midday, between fourth and fifth period, late-morning sun streamed through classroom doors jammed with students. The roar of the crowd was just about even with the rush of construction. I'd had two Motrin earlier, though, and my head wasn't hurting too bad.

I was leaving bio on my way to gym when Erica stopped me.

"Yo, Dunne!" she said as she came out of a classroom, smiling sweetly. "Is everyone gonna pass that algebra test or what?"

I wanted to say, Well, technically, we'd all have to be *taking* algebra to pass the test, and I, for instance, am in trig, but I didn't. Instead, I just said, "Hell yeah!" and fell into step beside her.

Maybe Vicky was right; maybe I am a coward.

"We on for tomorrow?" she asked, sounding a little nervous.

"About that, Erica—"

"Hold that thought," she said. As we walked, she took her book out and wrote in it. I was afraid for a second she was writing "Caleb Dunne will study with me," but I could tell, just from the movements of her pen, what she was writing. Only now she'd generously changed "I" to "everyone in the class" to match the group Crave.

"Haven't seen you do that in a while," I said, nudging her shoulder. "I have to tell you . . ."

Before I could finish, there was a loud hooting down the hall. Far off, people stopped in their tracks as their heads twisted to follow someone moving along at a full run. Whoever it was, judging from the way the crowd was splitting, he was headed our way.

"We did it! We did it!" someone screamed.

Among all the arms and legs of the Screech Neck student body, I made out a large male form running along, yipping and hollering, hands in the air like he'd just crossed the finish line at a marathon.

"We did it! We did it!"

It was Dylan.

Before he could run past us, I flagged him down.

"Dylan, what'd we do?"

He grinned at me, wild eyed. "Our new Crave, man, it worked! Everyone's passing the algebra test! Whooooooo-hoooo!"

"Wait a minute, wait a minute! The test isn't until Monday. How do you know everyone's going to pass?"

He could barely contain himself. "Eldridge was in a freaking car accident! He's out for at least a month! Everyone's taking Blubaugh's easy-ass test! It's a slam dunk! We did it!"

Then he started hooting and jumping up and down again.

Erica, meanwhile, looked like someone had punched her in the gut.

"Is he all right?" she asked softly.

I turned to Dylan. "Yo! Eldridge? He okay?"

But Dylan either didn't hear me or didn't want to. He just kept hooting and jumping. Then he ran down the hall, screaming, "We did it! We did it!"

We'd certainly done something.

- We're all upset about what happened to Mr. Eldridge, but Ethan wanted me to make sure everyone understands that we're not responsible. Mr. Eldridge chose to live as a very negative person, and negativity attracts negative events. Whether he realized it or not, he wanted his brakes to fail. His path brought him there. His choices. There is no reason any of us should feel bad about it. —Vicky

- I would still like the greatest gaming system in the world, the Xbox. A 733 MHz Intel main processor and 233 MHz graphics processor from nVidia create photorealistic graphics in real time. A huge hard drive stores saved games and characters, and a built-in Ethernet port enables super-fast multiplayer online gaming over a broadband Internet connection. —Landon

- I can't deal with this. Things are getting too freaky and people are getting hurt. I'm out of here. Patience and peace for everyone! —Will

- Ethan and Vicky are right. We should stop whining. The universe is a big and complicated place. What we want is part of that, but so is what Eldridge wanted for himself. So let's shut up and move on to our next Crave! I want to work on passing chemistry next. Mrs. Baxter was out last year with some kind of illness. Maybe she could have a relapse. —Jacob

- I still want my brother home. I'm ashamed to admit it, but I don't really care what it takes or what else it changes. He missed our last IM session and we haven't heard from him in a few days. Yesterday my mother was crying in the middle of the day. I want him home. —Alex

- I think deep down Mr. Eldridge was hoping for a wake-up call. He sure got one! Maybe when he comes back, he'll understand better how *The Rule* works. It's a blessing, really! We can't stop now! How about we turn the whole Screech Neck economy around by getting everyone to buy *The Rule of Won*? Me, I want to imanifest a whole flock of monarch butterflies outside my window every morning! —Grace

- Still no Porsche, but I have made a breakthrough. I understand now that it's not selfish to want things even though certain people might try to make me feel bad about it. I don't feel bad, I feel good, okay? I just want to feel good. Is that so wrong? —Colleen

- More than anything I have ever wanted, more deeply than

anything I have ever felt or imagined, I want yesterday not to have happened. —Erica

- Screw Eldridge. He had it coming. —Dylan

- I'm sorry the guy got hurt, but I'm glad to be part of this. If people feel bad about it, though, maybe we should make Eldridge's recovery our next Crave? Or at least send him a card? —Mike

- We've rebuilt half the school, handed a bunch of loser basketball players a winning game, and now we nearly killed a teacher. So why, why, why can't I get a freaking iPhone destroyed? I mean, Nicole got herself a new denim sleeve for the damn thing and she's parading it all over the place. I can't stand it! Why can't that phone get into a car accident already? —Sophia

- I don't care about the test. I don't care about this club. I don't care about the book. Mr. Eldridge almost died and it's as if I almost killed him. I want to have had nothing to do with this. —Erica

- We had a little gathering for Mr. Eldridge out in the woods. It began as a sort of get-well-soon party, then it got to be more party than get-well. There were some college kids who brought some contraband and were prepared to share. It was the greatest time in the world until the cops showed. I nearly broke my leg running away, but I imanifested and made it! —Jane

- Nothing happens if you don't want it to! I'm so proud of us I could burst. I feel like I know everyone in the school now, like we're all part of one big family. I even like being here more than at home. I think it's sad that some people still haven't caught on. —Olivia

- I've decided not to even show up for the algebra exam. It doesn't matter what it means. If this is what it takes to succeed in life, I don't want to succeed. —Erica

- Hooray for the Crave! And for Dylan and Mike for taking care of that a-hole in the cafeteria who was calling me gay. I know who I am and I am one of you! —Andrew

- Is it me or is it that lately the cafeteria food really doesn't seem so bad? I'm not saying it's like home-cooked, or even McDonald's, but I'm finding it distinctly tastier. Could this be yet another Crave we've brought to fruition, without even realizing it? —Benjamin

- I don't know if what happened with Mr. Eldridge was right or wrong, and I don't care that much. That girl from last week is pressing charges. My hearing's next week. With everything going crazy at home, I need this club badly just to get my mind off things. If we made a mistake, let's fix it. If we didn't, let's feel good about it. —Jeff

- I don't want to be me anymore. —Erica

- I don't think it was an accident. I think someone was trying to kill Mr. Eldridge, and I think it was that guy in the lunchroom. He knows I'm thinking he did it, and now he'll have to kill me to shut me up. I have ways of protecting myself, but I'm afraid when the time comes, I'll be too scared to use them. —Lauren

- I want all of you to go away. I want all of this to go away. I want to stop thinking about this. I want to stop thinking. I want to stop breathing. Where's Caleb? —Erica

- I don't like to interfere with this message board, especially since it's been growing so wonderfully on its own, but lately some of our members have been focusing on negative emotions, and I don't think that does any of us any good, least of all them. So, I'm sorry to say, I'm blocking further messages from Erica and Lauren. We can discuss this decision at the next Crave, and if it's clear they understand what we're about, I'll certainly restore their privileges. —Ethan

- It's great that the club is getting big and all, but for some people it makes it really hard to talk about certain other people because now those certain other people are members and listening in. So, I'm wondering if we can limit the membership or maybe have a separate meeting just with the original Cravers? —Kathleen

- With Mom in college and me looking after my kid sister, I really don't have the time for the club anymore. It's getting kind of crowded anyway. I promise I'll be chanting at home, though, so please stop asking. —Hailey

- I never realized how powerful this was and I now know more than ever that we have to be careful and responsible, and I feel kind of silly I ever asked for something like clothes. Everybody's talking about how fossil fuels are destroying the environment and causing wars and stuff, so why don't we focus on some kind of sun-driven alternative energy source? —Beth

- The new meeting room's great, but I think even it's going to be too packed next time. Do you think we should hold our next Crave in the auditorium? —Tom

- Of course we're all upset about what happened to Erica, but it's important to remind ourselves that her own decisions brought her to her suicide attempt. Her choices. Her path. There's no reason any of us should feel bad about it. —Vicky

Big, square thing, the county hospital, all brick and glass with a lot of dingy sky behind it. It was probably built by the same construction company handling the gym. The building, not the sky. Whatever. I was outside, my lazy ass on a bench. Erica Black was inside, in some room or ward, hooked up to all sorts of tubes, for all I knew, struggling to breathe, for all I knew. Dead, for all I knew.

I'd read her posts over the weekend and known something was up, but was too dense to guess what. At first I thought she'd just stayed home to mope in her dark place. I should have called, or at least posted something when she mentioned me by name, but I didn't.

Slacker, you know?

Yeah, right.

Rumors flew like crazy—she'd slit her wrists with a razor, taken a bottle of pills, thrown herself in front of a train, run a vacuum hose from the exhaust of her parents' car into the backseat, all of the above. Everyone seemed surprised that *I* didn't know more, because I was her best (and apparently only) friend.

One guy, Jim Pindell, made a wisecrack about how, because she was so pale to begin with, they couldn't tell if she was dead or not. I was about to punch him square in his big mouth, but he had a "1" pin on and Dylan and Mike were there.

They stepped between us real fast, like two fleshy tanks.

"Where's *your* pin?" Dylan asked, nodding at my empty collar.

"Out in the field. Maybe some bird ate it by now," I told him.

"Better get a new one," he said.

Mike was a touch friendlier. "Really, man, you should."

Dylan pressed his face close to mine. He'd had french toast for breakfast, judging by the smell. "Everyone's gonna pass the algebra test!"

The idiot didn't even realize the test had been canceled since Erica's suicide attempt.

I walked. Scurried, actually, to put as much distance as I could between us before someone spilled it to the great ape Kong that I'd quit the Crave.

My actual resignation was pretty anticlimactic. By third period the "S" word (Slacker) wasn't sitting too well, and I was thinking someone should do something, maybe even me. So I headed to the former office of *The Otus*. Ethan and Vicky were standing oh-so-close as they hung up a poster together and, just like that, I said, "I quit."

No big fanfare. Two little words. Ethan looked like he

pitied me. He mumbled something about having to choose my own path, like it was total news to me that I had free will. Vicky glared, like I was betraying her.

Ha. Me, betraying her.

I thought they should shut down the school and let us go home for the rest of the day. When they didn't, I took off on my own. Hooky's unusual for me. Breaking rules, you see, takes too much of an effort.

A bus ride or so later, I was sitting outside the hospital, too afraid to go in, too depressed and guilty to go home. I just stared at the building, wondering if it was going to fall down just because I was looking at it.

My brain kept drifting back to that girl on the Whirl-A-Gig, unbuckling herself and standing up, getting hurled from the ride, snapping her neck and dying. I pictured her blond and nasty, a real brat, someone you really wouldn't mind seeing die.

But she kept changing into Erica.

I might have stayed there all day, or gone the coward route and slunk home, but this couple in their late forties came out, he in a tweed jacket, she pale, with horn-rimmed glasses, both looking professorial, both looking sad and exhausted, both looking just enough like Erica for me to make the connection.

"I shouldn't have left my pills in that medicine cabinet," the woman said, her voice cracking into tears.

"Yes, a medicine cabinet is an absurd place for medicine," the man replied. "She's fine. She'll be fine. You heard the doctor," he said, putting his arm around her shoulder.

"It's my fault," she answered. "All my fault."

"Come, now, neither of us saw it coming. No one did."

"I knew how much she wanted that scholarship! I knew how that test was driving her crazy! I should've gotten her a tutor!"

"We couldn't afford it, Lisa," he said in a quiet voice. "And you're not the one who quit his job."

"Don't you start," she said. She kissed him on the cheek.

"She'll be fine," he said. "She'll be fine."

"We should go back."

"She's sleeping. Let's just get some coffee."

"To go?"

"Absolutely."

How about that? What with *The Rule* floating around so much lately, it was the first conversation in eons I'd heard where people were arguing about *taking* the blame for something that happened to someone else. I wanted to run up, introduce myself, and explain how it was really all *my* fault. Then maybe we could all hug. Yeah, I know, I hate group hugs, but sometimes you just need one.

It also made me feel so totally low about not going in, that as soon as they were out of sight, I got off my lazy ass and headed into the lobby.

Without even looking at me, the woman at the front desk asked, "Can I help you?"

"Erica Black."

She clicked a few keys. "Room 243A. But visiting hours are almost over."

"I won't be long. Please."

Now she did look up. Scanned me like I was a computer screen. I guess I passed whatever test she was giving, because she handed me a plastic visitor card.

The elevator opened out to a view of the nurses' station. That weird mix of cleaning and bodily fluids that only hospitals and school cafeterias have hit my nostrils.

The station nurse was so wrapped up in her dog-eared paperback that she ignored me. Other than that, it was pretty empty, except for one short, balding guy in a hospital gown who was leaning on the wall and sort of half sliding down the hall.

I didn't like looking at him—he'd been bruised pretty badly—but I didn't know if it was ruder to turn away or stare. The welts on his skin were a deep purple, almost like Barney the dinosaur. Just as I put a name to him, he spotted me.

So I said, cool as I could, "Hey, Mr. Eldridge. How's it going?"

"Dunne?" he answered, surprise replacing the pain on his face. He narrowed his eyes and gave me a purple smile. "Here to see *me*? Had no idea you cared."

"Uh . . ."

He laughed. "Relax. I know Ms. Black's here."

At least I was able to make him forget his troubles by being the target of his mockery.

"So, you doing better, Mr. E?"

"If healing hurts a lot, I'm doing great." He grimaced, then nodded curiously at my shirt. "Pin's gone. Come to your senses?"

"I guess."

"Not so dumb after all. And apparently not the slacker you like to think you are. It's harder to fight your friends than it is to fight city hall. Did you know our principal was wearing a *Rule of Won* pin when he came to visit me?"

"Wow."

"Oh, don't be surprised. Wyatt was always an idiot."

"I'm really glad you're okay, Mr. Eldridge."

"I believe you are. Thanks, Dunne. We'll talk again. You should visit your friend."

He hobbled through the nearest doorway, which, I figured, led to his room. What with most of the school so happy about his accident, I was thinking he must feel pretty alone. But when I peeked in after him, I saw stacks of cards, flowers, and balloons, which meant, I guess, that he wasn't so alone after all.

The last time I'd been in a hospital was when some old aunt of my mother's (Lydia?) was on her deathbed. It was a big deal for Mom that I go in and see this dying woman I barely knew. I was ten and totally refusing. Mom begged, whined, pleaded, and tried to bribe me. I could tell from her exasperated sighing she was just about to give up, when Joey grabbed my arm, yanked me inside, and croaked, "Say hello to your great-aunt."

It was a horror show. She was all wrinkled and yellow with a ton of tubes jabbed into various parts of her body. She never even opened her eyes while I was there, but Joey made me whisper to her anyway.

He saw how hard it was, but he didn't care. On the way

out, when I complained that she didn't even know I was there, he said, "It's not about her. It's about you. You can't make things go away just by ignoring them. The world won't change just because you don't feel like believing in it."

Joey, man. Someday, I'm going to write a book filled with quotes by him. Be more useful than *The Rule of Won,* I bet.

I was kind of wishing he was here with me now, just to yell at me that I wasn't ten anymore and Erica wasn't Aunt Lydia.

Room 243A was a double room. Whoever was closest to the door was hidden behind a curtain, except for their toes, which poked up through the blankets at the end of the bed, looking white, like the sheets.

It wasn't Erica. She was near the window. I had to wonder if that was smart, like, what if she wanted to jump or something? Then again, it was only one story down.

She lay with her head on three pillows, eyes closed, sleeping. The pillows looked stiff, and so did the pillowcases, sheets, and blankets. There were no tubes, just one little intravenous needle. The spot where it entered the back of her hand was covered up with tape. Under the blankets, her chest rose and fell.

I stood in the doorway, relieved she didn't look like a total mess, worried there might be some invisible brain damage or something.

Erica's chest heaved, then stopped moving. I was afraid she wasn't breathing anymore, but she let out a few short bursts of air from her nose and smiled. Something she was dreaming about struck her as funny, I guess.

A nurse wheeled a cart behind me, making me step forward

into the room to get out of the way. I didn't hear myself make any noise, but Erica did, because her eyelids fluttered open.

"Caleb?" she said softly.

"Hey," I said. "Pills, huh? I thought drugs cause cramp. Like that poem."

"They do indeed."

"But you're okay?"

She blinked and stretched a little, then wriggled under her sheets. "Yep. Except for the *Girl, Interrupted* thing."

"Right. That. Which was about . . . what?"

"I just . . . I just really wanted to get into Hampshire Arts."

"And attempted suicide was on the application?"

"I misread the form."

"No, really," I said. "Was it guilt because you thought you caused Eldridge's accident?"

She looked away and wrinkled her lips. "More that part of me didn't mind if I *did* cause the accident. When I realized that, I felt like I didn't deserve much of anything."

"Like breathing?"

"Like breathing."

I pulled up a chair and sat in it backward. "First of all, you never wished for Mr. Eldridge to get hurt. You haven't got a mean bone in your body. Second of all, I'm starting to think *The Rule of Won* is totally whack. You didn't make anything happen. It just did."

"That's what Mr. Eldridge said."

"You talked to him about it?"

"Who better? I apologized."

"Gutsy."

"He said there was nothing to apologize for."

"See? And he's a teacher. He knows stuff."

She smiled a little.

"But, Erica, you were freaking out way before Eldridge's accident. What's so damn important about a school? I mean, it's just a school, right?"

She leaned back and looked at the ceiling. "I guess it's hard for you to understand . . ."

"Because I'm a slacker? Because—"

"No. Because you've lived here all your life. You're used to it. I just never felt like I could be myself in Screech Neck. It's like I'm constantly surrounded by things trying very hard to make me not me. I just thought maybe at an arts college, I could be myself again, or maybe for the first time."

I leaned in and nudged her shoulder. "Erica, wherever you wind up, I'm very, very sure you have been and always will be Erica."

I wasn't sure where that came from. She gave me that weird half smile she gets sometimes.

"You don't hate me, do you, Caleb?"

"No. Why would I?"

"Or think I'm totally crazy."

"Well, you did try to kill yourself. That does take a few points off the sane score."

"I won't do it again."

"Promise?"

She looked me in the eyes. "Yes. It wasn't nearly as romantic or peaceful as I thought. Lots of crying and screaming, mostly, which I suppose means I never really wanted to die in the first place. I think it was just what they call a desperate cry for help."

"Okay. But next time maybe you could just say, 'help'?"

She crossed her arms over her chest. I was worried about that intravenous thing, but it didn't seem to bother her. "And if I did, would you?"

"Would I what?"

"Help."

"Uh . . . does it involve algebra?"

"Not right now, no."

"Then . . . yeah."

I shifted uncomfortably, then put my hand on hers. I expected it to be cold, because the room was chilly and her skin was always so pale, but even her fingertips felt warm. I was worried it'd feel strange, but it didn't. It felt good.

We didn't say anything else until the station nurse came in and said it was time for me to go. I was a little relieved. I was happy to sit with Erica, but her parents would be back and I didn't feel like dealing with them, what with not knowing what to say and not wanting them to grill me or treat me like I was her boyfriend.

By the time I made it back into the hall, the elevator was opening and I heard some people talking. Worried it was the Blacks, I slipped into the stairwell.

And there I heard a voice. "Are they okay?"

On the next landing up a girl stood, maybe middle-school

age. She had on these weird, tight stockings, one pink, one green. I wasn't sure who she was talking to.

"Are they okay?" she asked again. "Erica Black and Mr. Eldridge?"

Turns out she was talking to me.

She spoke as if she were entitled to an answer. Her tone reminded me of someone.

"Uh . . . Eldridge is pretty bruised, but Erica seems fine. Do I . . . do I know you?"

An ever so slightly smug smile spread on her face. That looked familiar, too.

"My name's Alyssa," she said. "Alyssa Skinson."

Of course. That's who she reminded me of. Ethan.

"Oh. I'm—"

"Caleb Dunne. My brother talks about you."

"Okay. I saw some of your drawings. You're good."

She smiled more genuinely. "Thanks. Ethan thinks they make things happen."

"No kidding. Do you?"

She shook her head and looked a little sad. "No way. It's just coincidence, but he doesn't believe me because of that book. He's changed since he read it. I thought maybe if I helped him a little, he'd change back, but he's only gotten worse."

"Hard to believe he was ever better."

"He was. He doesn't like you, by the way. He didn't like you before you quit, but now he really doesn't. None of them do. It was only a few hours ago, but some of them are already talking about you on the board."

"Ethan lets you read the message board?"

She raised an eyebrow. "He doesn't *let* me. He just leaves his passwords lying around sometimes."

Out of the blue, I asked, "Alyssa, do you think you could help me?"

"I won't draw any pictures for you, if that's what you mean."

"I don't know what I mean," I admitted. "Any idea what 'Vanuatu' means? Or *Mondo Cane*? *Mondo Cane*'s an old documentary, but I can't rent it anywhere. I can order it online but I don't have the money."

"No," she said. "Sorry." She turned, ready to leave. "I have to get back now."

I wanted something more from her, what, I couldn't say. I didn't think I should tell her I'd eavesdropped on that call with Ethan, but I wanted to hint that I knew something more was up, so I blurted out with my usual subtlety, "I think people should study on their own, too."

She spun back and eyed me. "If that documentary's old, it could be on tape. Do you have one of those VHS players?"

"My grandfather does. Still won't switch to DVD."

She nodded, then walked off.

It was dark by the time I made it home. The sky was as clear as it gets, and you could see one or two stars poking up above the buildings, like little Christmas lights. It was almost curfew for me, and I was looking forward to getting some sleep.

Outside my building, on the stone stoop, four shadowy figures loitered. When the tallest spotted me, they all turned to stare, like I was what they'd been waiting for.

I was afraid it was Dylan, Mike, and the other Crave jocks, ready to stab me to death with a new "1" pin. I was too tired to run, though.

As I got closer, even though they were trying as hard as they could to look tough, I had to breathe a sigh of relief.

"Moore, Guy, Drik, and Mason," I said, walking up. "What the hell are you—"

"Shh!" Moore said, waving me closer. He had a black case in his hands.

Drik, who had on a scarf and long coat that made him look like a Dr. Who wannabe, looked around nervously as Mason hissed, "Keep it down." A thick kerchief covered most of her head, almost like a burka, only there were little Pokemon printed on it.

"Fine," I whispered. "What's up with your bad secretive selves?"

Guy had on a real black leather jacket, and I had to admit, he almost pulled off the tough-guy thing. He looked me over like he was frisking me with his eyes.

"It's true. The pin's gone," he said to the others.

"You did quit," Moore said with a thin smile.

"Were you at the hospital? How's the girl?" Mason asked.

"Erica? Fine. She's okay. What's going on? Finally going to tell me what 'Vanuatu' means?"

Moore handed Drik the case. "Something big is going

down. We want to make sure someone other than us knows about it."

"Someone we can trust. In case something happens to us," Guy intoned mysteriously.

"Happens to you? The only thing that would happen to you guys is you'd get abducted by aliens at a *Battlestar Galactica* convention."

All four eyed me. "This is serious," Moore said. *"Serious."* He said it slowly, to make it clear they wouldn't put up with any more geek jokes. "It's about what happened to Mr. Eldridge."

I heard a laptop hard drive whir to life. Drik was booting Moore's rig.

"You mean the accident?"

Moore's face remained unmoved. "The police don't think it was an accident."

I furrowed my brow so hard I felt the skin at the back of my head tighten and pull. "Please. How do *you* know what the police think?"

"I maybe . . . sort of . . . hacked into their system," Drik said as he spun the laptop toward me.

My eyes went wide. There on the screen, in glorious black and white, was a blurry video image of someone's driveway.

Moore put his finger near the screen. "This is the footage the police are looking at from Mr. Eldridge's security camera."

My mouth got as round as a Cheerio. "How did you . . . ?"

"We just did. Watch."

Drik clicked and a figure dressed in black pants, shirt, and ski mask climbed over Mr. E's fence. The figure fidgeted under the car, then slipped back over the fence. The clip was on a loop, and after a second, it played again.

"Holy crap!" I shouted.

"Indeed. No magic there. His brake line was cut," Moore said. "Stupid amateur job. The police have no idea who that was, yet, but we're going to do a big story about it in the school paper for our first issue."

My eyes were glued to the screen as the figure slid under the car again. "Who is it?" I asked. "Dylan's psychotic, but he's way bigger than that. Wait. Can you zoom in on his feet?"

"His feet? Why?" Drik asked.

"Tell you in a minute."

Moore nodded and Drik made a little square around the feet by dragging his finger across the touchpad, then clicked on a magnifying-glass icon a few times. The picture got bigger, but it was also getting all blocky. Even so, I thought I could see them pretty clearly: two shoelaces glowing so brightly they looked as if they'd been bleached.

It was Ethan.

Silly me. I was thinking we should go to the police, what with Ethan having attempted the murder of Mr. Eldridge and all.

When I suggested it, Drik immediately got a wild psycho look in his eyes and screeched, "No!" so loudly it echoed down the whole block. "Do you have any idea how illegal it is to hack into police files?"

I reached up to pat him on the shoulder. "A little perspective, okay? I'm pretty sure they'd make an exception if you helped solve an attempted murder."

"First off, *I* didn't say it was Ethan, you did. You say they're shoelaces, but at that low resolution they could just be lines on his sneaker, or shadows from the fence," Drik said.

"Really? What about the rest of you? Don't any of you see the shoelaces?"

They all shrugged. The only real response I got was from Moore, who mumbled something like, "It really *is* hard to tell."

"Fine!" I said. "I'll go to the cops myself!"

Guy, who'd been leaning against the concrete banister,

pushed himself up straight. "Let's say you're right, it *is* Ethan. Hey, I think it probably is, but do you really think the police will believe you about two blurry shoelaces when the student you're accusing just stole your girlfriend? They're still looking at you cross-eyed over the gym collapse."

"Yeah," I said. "Thanks for reminding me how *that* little problem could've been solved if you Pulitzer Prize winners had managed to publish one lousy issue!"

Moore shrugged guiltily. "The bottom line is we can't prove it's Ethan. And the only way we got Drik to show us their files in the first place was by swearing we wouldn't go directly to the cops with anything we found."

"Oh, great. Just great," I said. "So what do we do?"

A low wind whipping around her headscarf, Mason exhaled through her mouth. "We can try to force the issue. We'll finish our exposé, tell people how the grant was publicized the week before, how it was common knowledge Regis was having a flu epidemic . . ."

"And," Moore added, "how an anonymous witness *thinks* they saw Ethan Skinson running away from Mr. Eldridge's home the night of the accident, which is pretty much true. That may bring out more witnesses."

"Just as long as no one mentions the security video," Drik said.

"Look, I hate to be the one to point this out, *again*, but you've been working on that issue for months. With Eldridge in the hospital, you don't even have an adviser. How are you actually going to print something now?"

Moore stiffened. "We still have access to the office. We'll put it together after school tomorrow. Marathon session. Faking a purchase order to pay for the printing should be easy enough. We can have it online by midnight, and the print version all over school by morning. Fast enough for you?"

"And what are you going to do when the cops ask for the name of your witness?" I asked. "Or the Cravers show up to kick your asses for accusing their glorious leader?"

"Reporters never reveal sources. We'll say our witness is afraid of the Crave and won't come forward. The police probably haven't released the tape because it's so blurry, but this may make them think twice. At least it'll come out that Eldridge was attacked," Moore said.

"Caleb's right, though," Guy said. "There'll be major blowback from the Cravers."

"Which is, like, more than half the school," I mumbled. "And you don't even need half the school for trouble. All you need is Dylan."

Everyone got real quiet after that. A few of them looked like they were going to start sentences, but no one got a word out, until finally I said, "Look, Ethan's a major asshole. I'll do anything I can to help you take him down. I don't care if the plan's stupid or not. At least it's a plan."

Drik slapped his hand against his shoulder, then stuck his arm out at an angle. "We who are about to die, salute you, Caesar."

"Dunne, we could use your help putting it together," Moore said. "Providing an anonymous insider perspective . . ."

"Whatever," I answered. "I'm tired. I'll see you tomorrow after school. Bring your running shoes."

When I finally got inside, Joey was sprawled on the couch, reading *The Rule of Won*. He looked up at me when I came in and shook his head.

"This is one steaming load of crap," he said.

"Yeah," I said as I closed the door.

"The girl worth it?"

"Turns out, no."

He sat up. "Then what'd you read it for?"

"How else was I going to figure out it was a load of crap?"

He laughed. "It only took me the first page. Everything else okay?"

I thought for a second I could tell him about Ethan, but really, what could he do?

"Yeah, fine."

He gave me a classic GP Joey look. "Why're you lying?"

"I'm not!"

It was a reflexive response, but once I'd said it, I felt like I should stick to it.

There was no snappy comeback. He looked hurt.

Trying to change the subject, I asked, "How's business?"

He narrowed his gaze and said, in a slightly higher-pitched voice that I think was supposed to be an imitation of mine, "Yeah, fine."

I knew what I was supposed to say next. I was supposed to say, "Why're you lying?" But I didn't. I just headed into my room.

I had one hell of a time trying to get to sleep. The only thing that calmed me was remembering that Erica seemed okay, and was probably better off being out of school right now.

By the time I crawled into the kitchen to make myself breakfast, I was still thinking about asking Joey's advice, but he'd already left.

Mom was still there, though. The sweet smell of brown-and-serve sausage filled the kitchen, and I heard the sizzle of frying eggs. She was making me breakfast.

With our schedules clashing, I hadn't seen her for days. It dawned on me that while I'd been spending my time chanting for a murderous psycho, she had been working like crazy to pay the bills. I felt not so much stupid as *guilty*, like I should have been helping, or, God forbid, working myself, or at least focusing on school like she wanted me to, or at least making *her* breakfast.

The feeling worsened as I rode the bus alone. When I got to school, I felt like everyone just somehow magically knew I was involved in a plan to blow the whistle on their beloved Crave leader.

The stray looks kids gave me in the halls seemed piercing. Landon pointedly ignored me. At least Dylan didn't come rushing up for a chant. When I passed him in the hall, he just touched two fingers to his eyes, then pointed at the spot on my collar where the pin used to be.

At lunch, I felt like a rat wandering into an aviary full of starving owls. Ethan, Vicky, Dylan, Mike, and Grace were all at the same table, hunched over and whispering. I couldn't take it. I just grabbed an apple, turned around, and sat in the library pretending to read a magazine.

The rest of the day, wherever I went, I swore I could hear people whispering. I wanted to grab a random Craver and tell them exactly what was going on, but aside from getting Drik into trouble, I wasn't sure they'd believe me. Some of them probably wouldn't believe anything except what Ethan told them.

Isn't that my wallet in your hand, Ethan? With my money and my ID in it?

Uh, nope!

My mistake. It must be yours.

The second the last bell rang, I was out of the classroom, eager to reach the trailers without being seen. As I raced down the hall, I kept looking over my shoulder, watching people spill out of the rooms, making sure no one was eyeing me. I figured I was home free until I rounded the corner that led to the rear doors.

Dylan, Mike, and some new, similarly stocky friend of theirs were there.

I seized up, just for a second. I figured it would look like I was up to something if I reversed course, so I decided to walk right past them. Yeah, right.

"Going somewhere, Dunne?" Dylan said, stepping in front of me.

I looked at him. Actually, I looked at his chest.

"You hear the bell?" I said as calmly as I could. "School's over. I'm going home."

"You always go out the back?" the new one said.

They couldn't possibly know about the newspaper meeting. *Could* they?

I shrugged in a really exaggerated way. "Sometimes."

Dylan poked me on the shirt, right where the pin used to be. His finger was as strong as the rest of him looked.

"A lot of people are disappointed you quit," he said.

"Yeah, well, I'm disappointed a lot more people didn't quit the club after Erica tried to kill herself."

"What is she, your girlfriend?"

"Not exactly," I said. "But she's a friend."

"She's a crazy bitch," Dylan said. "She was going to get exactly what she wanted, but she couldn't deal with it, so she tried to bring the rest of us down with her whining. I mean, so what if Eldridge had an accident?"

The mysterious third person nodded. "Want to make an omelet, you gotta crack some eggs."

Not knowing when to shut up, I opened my big mouth and said, "It wasn't an accident."

They all looked at one another. I was thinking I'd opened up a whole can of worms, but Dylan just sneered and said, "Of course it wasn't an accident. We imanifested it."

Right.

Remembering Mike as the vaguely reasonable one, I turned to him. "You guys going to beat me up for quitting, or can I get going?"

Mike nodded at Dylan. "Let him go."

Dylan twisted sideways, giving me just enough space to get through the door.

"Yeah," he said as I passed. "We can always imanifest an accident for him, too."

When I reached the parking lot, I wanted to look back to make sure they weren't watching, but I didn't want them to know I was worried about them, so I kept walking until I could duck behind one of the trailers. There, I stopped and peeked back. The rear door was swinging shut, as if someone had just opened it, but there was no one in sight. That didn't mean anything. Lots of kids left the school that way. Sure enough, a few seconds later, the door swung open and a few stumbled out, no members of *The Rule* goon squad visible.

I told myself they'd just happened to see me and wanted to scare me. It was probably nothing, so I didn't even mention it when I entered the moldy old trailer where the newspaper club now met.

Moore and Mason tapped away at laptops. Two huge bottles of Diet Pepsi were open on either side of them and a plastic bag sat between them, chips, pretzels, and other munchies jutting from the top. Drik was pulling a sheet of paper from the printer.

Even from the door, I could read the headline: "The Rule of Lies."

Guy wasn't there, but I didn't think much of that yet. Didn't have much of a chance to, since Moore nearly shoved me into a chair and started grilling me about the Crave. Who spoke? What did they say? How are things run? The answer to most of his questions was Ethan.

"It was pretty much by the book until I staged my little rebellion," I told him. "If Ethan hadn't canceled my password, I could log you guys into the message board."

Mason shook her head. "Don't worry. We've been following that for weeks."

"Oh. Drik get you in there, too?"

When I said that, they all looked at me like I should already know. Drik said, "Someone sent us a password anonymously."

"We thought it was you," Moore said.

I shook my head. "Nice. Someone else is on our side, huh?"

"Maybe," Mason said as she went back to her typing. "Where's Guy? He should be here by now."

Moore flipped open an old battered cell.

"Guy, we're here, where are you?" he said. His face got funny as he listened to the response. "What do you mean? You're our Hercules, man! You wimping out on us? Now? I don't believe you! Half the articles are yours! But . . ."

Moore snapped his phone shut. "He's not coming. Says he doesn't think it's a good idea anymore, that we should let the police handle it."

Drik and Mason looked stricken. "But he spent a month on the history piece."

"He said we could run it, but without his name."

"Wow," Mason said, shaking her head. "Wow."

Moore slumped back in his chair as if someone had let all the air out of him.

Drik's shoulders twitched. "He didn't tell the police about the video, did he?"

"Hey, calm down," I said. "He's probably just scared. Don't know if you've noticed, but the Crave's scary." If I was the most level-headed of the bunch of us, we were in big trouble.

"Yeah," Moore said absently. "Freaking Vanuatu."

"Aghh! Would you tell me what that means already?" I said. "It's driving me nuts."

He shook his head. "Work for it. It's not hard to find out if you try." He turned to the others. "Still in?"

They nodded.

Despite the growing creepiness that hung over the trailer, especially as it got darker and the air grew thicker with mold, we all pitched in. Once Moore ran out of things to ask me, I was handed a copy of what they had so far and asked to proofread it.

It was pretty good stuff, laying out the facts about how what the Crave had accomplished wasn't so much miraculous as occasionally criminal. There was also an editorial piece on how destructive the basic ideas of *The Rule* are, how it blames victims for their misfortune, creating an excuse not to help anyone, even an excuse for oppressing people (because, after all, you could only oppress someone who *wanted* to be oppressed, so why not oppress them?), how it refuses to acknowledge that sometimes tough choices have to be made in life, how it ridicules the notion of self-sacrifice and holds up greed—the right to get whatever you want, whenever you want it—as some kind of ideal.

I even liked Guy's history piece. He traced the supposedly shocking and new ideas in *The Rule of Won* back to two books that first appeared at the turn of the twentieth century: *Thought Vibration or the Law of Attraction in the Thought World* from 1906 and *The Science of Getting Rich*, published in 1910. That second one says the universe is made of a kind of thinking material that picks up on your desires and eventually manifests them. It, at least, also says you have to take some *action* to get what you want. A hundred years later, it seems we've moved backward.

There was even a fun article by Moore about how gullible people are. It told about this Web site that warned about the dangers of a compound called dihydrogen monoxide. This kid in California collected signatures for a petition to ban it. Only dihydrogen monoxide is actually just H_20, water. Even so, the kid got hundreds of signatures, and no one bothered to check their facts, preferring to rely on word of mouth.

That made me realize, with some annoyance, the point Moore was trying to make about me and "Vanuatu." He could tell me it meant whatever he wanted it to, lie through his teeth about it, unless I found out for myself.

Either that or he just liked yanking my chain.

And no, they didn't publish the article about me and the building collapse. I didn't mention it, since it seemed relatively unimportant.

When I finished, I noticed Moore, Drik, and Mason all tapping their feet, waiting. Thinking they wanted my opinion, I smiled and said, "This is great!"

Mason snapped her fingers a few times in rapid succession. "Yeah, yeah, yeah, any typos?"

"Way to take a compliment," I said, handing her the pages. I'd found only one or two words I thought were misspelled, and I wasn't sure about those.

"We're all a little tense," Moore said. As he reached for the Diet Pepsi, I noticed his hand was shaking.

"The sooner we're out of here, the better," Drik said.

I half laughed. "What are you afraid of *now*? The problem's tomorrow morning when everyone reads this."

Drik looked up and away. "Good point. My parents let me take a mental health day once a month. I've been saving a few . . ."

Moore turned to Mason. "Are we finished?"

She pressed a single key. "Yep. Just e-mailed it with our fake purchase order. By the time we get to the Regis Pronto Print, it may even be ready. Then we just leave it in the front hall and the janitors will distribute it around five A.M."

"I'll help with pickup, but tomorrow is mental health day," Drik said. "Mental health *week* if I can manage it."

"Fine. You and Mason get going. I'll stay and post online," Moore said.

"You sure?" Drik asked. "That could wait. You could do it from home."

Moore shook his head. "We've been waiting long enough."

Mason scooped up one of the humongous bottles of diet soda on her way out. "I'll drink, you drive," she said to Drik as they disappeared out the door.

Moore waited until he heard their car pull out, then

clicked UPLOAD on his laptop and watched the bar indicator rise to 100 percent.

"And that is that," he said. He blew some air between his pursed lips, leaned back in the squeaky desk chair he was in, and eyed me until I said, "What?"

"Thanks for helping," he said. "I misjudged you."

"Moore?"

"What?"

"*The Rule of Won*, you think it's *total* garbage?"

He made a face. "I said I was okay with positive thinking. If you believe you *can* get something, your brain will be looking for ways to get it. Of course that'll make it more likely you will. But that's not magic, it's just tricking yourself into doing a little extra work."

I pressed him on the point. "But even you can't say it *never* happens just the way the book says?"

He rolled his eyes and reached for the remaining soda bottle. "You mean is it *possible* some freaky mutant out there in the big bad cosmos has the ability to manifest his thoughts the way the superhero Frozone generates ice from moisture in the air?"

"If you put it that way, it sounds stupid, but yeah."

He shrugged, drained the bottle, then smacked his lips. "Anything's *possible*." He slid out of his chair and stretched. "Man, do I have to piss."

"Probably all that dihydrogen monoxide you're consuming."

He laughed. First time I had seen him actually laugh. He paused at the door.

"You're not so bad, Dunne. Wait with my laptop a minute. I'll walk you to the bus after I hit the head."

He slipped out. I wanted to wildly exhale now that all the work was finished, but didn't want to wind up inhaling too much mold. Instead, I amused myself by poking through the junk food bag and seeing if there was anything left worth chewing on.

Moore, it was turning out, wasn't so bad either. Alden.

I'd just put my hands on a half-empty (or half-full if you want to think positive) bag of Pringles when I heard a cry from outside.

"Caleb!"

It was Moore's voice. Maybe he was having trouble opening the door. It had gotten stuck on me the last time I'd gone out.

"What?" I shouted back. Nothing. There was a thud as something heavy pressed against the door. "Moore?"

I heard scuffling, a low moan, then a few rapid thuds.

"Moore?" I yelled, heading for the door. I pushed, but it wouldn't budge.

"Caleb!" Moore screamed. Then came a few more thuds, which I realized sounded like someone getting punched. "Help!"

More thuds.

"Hey!" I shouted, shoving my shoulder against the door. "Hey!"

It gave an inch and I caught a glimpse of a black sweater on the other side. Someone was holding it shut.

"Caleb!" Moore said again, only this time it sounded more like a cry.

I rammed into the door as hard as I could. The metal frame bent as I slammed it, but whoever was on the other side was bigger and stronger than me or the door.

Moore moaned now, occasionally making a pained gasp or gurgling noise as the thuds and punches continued.

Shoulder stinging from smashing the door, I headed for one of the small trailer windows and shoved it open as far as it would go. Outside, in the yellow parking-lot lights, I could make out two large, dark figures hovering over a fallen Moore, punching and kicking him. A third was leaning into the trailer door.

"Hey!" I screamed, as loudly as I could. "Help! Help!"

They stopped and turned toward me. "Help!" I shouted again. Moore was rolling on the ground in something wet. I couldn't tell if it was a puddle or his blood.

I climbed half out the window into the cold night air, yelling, "Help!"

It was an old trick Joey had taught me, one you use only when you're really desperate. Muggers and bullies don't want attention, so if you scream as loudly as you can, sometimes it scares them off. Sometimes.

They hesitated, not sure whether to come for me or not. I let out a really loud "Help!" that echoed all the way across the parking lot and nearly destroyed my throat. All three hightailed it out of there.

I could've used the door now, but I was halfway out the window and worried about Moore, so I kept moving, dropped to the ground, and raced over.

"You all right?" I asked as I kneeled next to him.

"No," he groaned. I put my hand down in the wetness that was around him and held it up into the haze from a streetlight. Cold, dirty water, not blood.

As he kept moaning, I pulled him out of the puddle, onto his back, and into the light for a better look. Mostly he seemed dazed, but a few gashes on his face were oozing lightly.

"Did you get a look at them?"

"No. See maks, just life Eevan inna bideo."

It took me a second to realize he was saying, "Ski masks, just like Ethan in the video," but he was having trouble speaking. That's when I noticed his mouth was open and his jaw looked kind of funny. You could see his tongue sort of lolling around in there as little puffs of water vapor spewed out with each short breath. Gross. I didn't know if his jaw had been broken or dislocated or what.

Afraid to move him any more, I slipped his cell phone out of his pocket.

"I'm calling an ambulance," I told him.

"Rearry? Am I dat bag?" he said, still looking dazed but genuinely surprised.

"Dude, your tongue is swelling up, and your jaw isn't moving right," I said as I dialed. "I think that was Dylan and Mike. The Crave Gestapo. They were hanging around, trying to muscle me when I got out of school. Maybe they saw the newspaper on the Web already?"

"Banuatu," Moore muttered, his eyes rolling into the back of his head. He looked like he was passing out.

"Crap, Moore! Why the hell can't you just *tell* me what it means?"

His eyelids fluttered and he lapsed into unconsciousness.

He could be such a pain in the ass.

- I'll never understand what's wrong with some people. Are they really so petty and jealous that we're doing well, that we found something to believe in, that we're happy changing the world for the better, that they have to try to tear it down with a bunch of lies? Stooping to trying to blame Ethan for a car accident? Ethan? Please. And they won't even name whoever supposedly saw him? Their minds are so small they have to come up with some tiny explanation that doesn't rock their world. I say our next Crave should be devoted to making these pathetic people see some reality. —Colleen

- The rest of the paper was stupid, too. How do they really know this dihydrogen monoxide stuff *isn't* a threat to people's health? Who has the right to say I'm gullible just because I wonder about things like that? Maybe there *should* be a ban. There should be a ban on dihydrogen monoxide and hate speech like in that paper. —Mike

- I didn't do it, but anyone who goes around making fun of people's beliefs deserves a broken jaw. Screw Moore, he had it coming. We'll be just fine. —Dylan

- It doesn't seem right to me that my brother is thousands of miles away risking his life for freedom, fighting for the rights of idiots like Alden Moore who think they can just trash whatever someone else is trying to build. I don't think Moore should have been beaten up, but I'm having a real hard time feeling bad about it. —Alex

- OMG, I can't believe it. Jasper Trelawney talks all about stuff like this in *The Rule*! For centuries people have been working in secret conspiracies to suppress knowledge of *The Rule*, to keep people down, uninformed, enslaved. Now we're seeing it firsthand! I'm not worried, because if each of us just imanifests a little bit each day, that embarrassing excuse for a newspaper and the people who made it will just vanish from the face of the earth! —Grace

- They don't thank us when things go right, but they blame us if someone gets hurt! Get real! Just because some bozos beat up that guy doesn't make us responsible! And Nicole, she gets this one tiny freaking nick on her iPhone that you can barely see unless you've got a high-powered lamp and a magnifying glass, and she blames me! Just because I happened to be standing near her precious device during art with a matte knife! We *all* had matte knives! It was art! —Sophia

- I was totally grounded after my parents found out about that get-well party, so I won't make the Craves for a while. I'm not even supposed to be online, but I read that stinking newspaper and heard about the attack and I wanted you all to know I'm with you forever. My vision's a little blurry lately, even when I'm sober! But, some blood tests are coming back next week. So how about a little imanifesting for my health? Keep a good thought, because, you know the rule, it's the thought that counts! ☺ —Jane

- Mr. Eldridge, Erica Black, Alden Moore. It's real eye-opening to see what happens to people who try to oppose *The Rule*. I know some kids are starting to think twice about the Crave, but I think it's time to start realizing that you're either on the side of the universe or against it. —Jacob

- I love you all so much, I really hate to see us attacked like this when all we've done is help. We've done such big things for this school, but if some of the kids are so ungrateful, maybe we should start thinking more about ourselves, and maybe imanifest, like, a winning lottery ticket for the Crave so we can all move away and live like one big family where no one will bother us. —Olivia

- I would no longer like the Xbox. What I would like now is the Xbox 360 Elite System, with a premium black finish and three powerful core processors capable of producing the best in HD entertainment (up to 1080p, like any Xbox 360), 16:9 cinematic aspect ratio, anti-aliasing for smooth textures, full surround sound, HDMI output, and DVD playback with upscaling capabilities right out of the box. —Landon

- It's really important that we stick together. Those newspaper geeks are trying to get some kind of investigation going, and if the police do start asking questions, we have to sound like we know what we're talking about. —Andrew

- So, somehow, in some way, we must have wanted this to happen, right? Does that mean only good will come of it, like it'll lead us down an even truer path, or does it mean some of us are secretly negative, working against the Crave without realizing it? If they are, we've got to find out who they are and stop them. —Benjamin

- The judge let me off with some lame education course and community service. I was all jazzed about that when I heard about the paper and the accusations. Wow. Don't know where to start. Maybe it's like an ocean wave, after we all got washed in the abundance of the universe, the water is sucking itself back in for an even bigger wave. So it looks dry right now, but we're about to be deluged in a major way. Hang on for an even better ride! —Jeff

- Now more than ever I think the original Cravers should be meeting separately so we can discuss what's going on. Maybe I'm paranoid, but I think my ex is stalking me and should be, like, arrested or something. The book says everything's connected, so that must have something to do with this and maybe together we can work out how. —Kathleen

- Please everyone, try not to panic. This will pass, you'll see. Old news in a few weeks. There's so many better things we could focus our energy on, like helping biodiesel come to Screech Neck. —Beth

- I did a rough count, and it looks like most of the seniors and at least half the juniors are wearing pins these days. I bet the same is happening in high schools all over the country, so really, what's going to stop us? —Tom

- Thanks for letting me back, guys, especially now that it seems like all my paranoia was on the mark. We know *The Rule*, we use it. Forces are lining up against us like crazy. I wouldn't even trust the police. Maybe this is like the End Times that Nostradamus and the Bible talk about. We have to imanifest some major protection for ourselves. I'll post if my dreams tell me anything else. —Lauren

- We were all terribly disappointed by the vicious and horrible lies some sadly misinformed students put out about Ethan and our Crave yesterday. As your student body president, I've scheduled an appointment with Dr. Wyatt to discuss it in detail.

Ethan's been talking with his father about filing a lawsuit. We already know the students were operating without an official adviser, and they may have broken some other rules as well. If you see copies of the paper in the school, feel free to toss them in the trash. Meanwhile, keep your cool, hold your head high. *The Rule* and this Crave rock! —Vicky

The interrogation room was tiny, just big enough for a table and two chairs. It may have been built to psychologically defeat a suspect, but that night I think it was the police who were defeated.

"You sure that's all?" the grizzly Detective Somebody or other asked. I hadn't caught his name and he hadn't bothered repeating it. We were both tired, but he was tired the way only middle-aged people get. He had wrinkles under his eyes so thick you could wedge a dime in there and I bet it'd stay put. He also hadn't shaved in a day or so.

When I didn't answer right away, he raised his eyes a little. I imagined the dime plopping out.

Had to say something. Didn't *want* to lie. I wanted to say, "Hell yeah, I recognized Ethan's shoelaces in the security video and he's a freaking psycho, so you should just drive over to his house and arrest him or at least shoot him."

But Detective What's-His-Name already hadn't particularly

believed me when I'd said it was Dylan and Mike who attacked Moore. I got a lot of, "You see their faces? Can you swear to that in court?"

To which, of course, I had to say no.

At times, it was almost like he thought *I'd* attacked Moore. He knew about me and the gym collapse in January and didn't have the benefit of Moore's research. Far as he knew, Moore was the guy who turned me in, so why should I be trying to help him?

If I'd told the truth, he would have thought I was lying, so I lied.

"That's all," I said. "That's all."

He sighed one of those twenty-minute sighs adults seem so good at, like their lungs have a slow leak from having to deal with us delinquents. But really, I think he was relieved we'd both be able to go home now. "You remember anything else, you let us know."

I never knew police detectives actually said that.

Mom and Joey were waiting in the hall. Mom was nearly in tears, saying mostly, "Oh my God" over and over and wiping my face with a wet handkerchief. Apparently I'd bruised my cheek on the way out the window, and in her panic, she thought she could rub the black and blue mark off. I didn't have the heart to tell her she was hurting me.

Joey played it silent, letting Mom go on and on about how bad that school was and so on and so forth. After she went to bed (had to get up at five for work, they were doing inventory), Joey and I were alone in the living room. I expected him to smack me for getting in trouble again, but he didn't.

"You okay?" he asked in an unusual display of outright sympathy.

"Yeah."

"The kids who beat up your friend, you get 'em?" He clenched his fists, to make sure I knew what "get 'em" meant.

"No," I said. "There were three, and they were big and fast."

"So use a piece of pipe. I'll get you one at the shop."

"Joey! No! Come on. Like that would be right?"

He shook his head and sighed like the detective. "Would've been in my day, but they keep changing the rules."

He grabbed my shoulder tightly, like he was trying to remind me how strong he was. Then he went to sleep himself.

I couldn't tell which was more depressing—the time I spent in the police station, the few hours I spent the next morning in the hospital visiting Moore, Erica (and yeah, Mr. Eldridge), or the rest of that day, when I returned to school.

Late November now, it was seriously colder outside and the heat had finally kicked in. The minute I pushed open the front doors to SNH warm air swarmed around me, hitting my face, shoulders, and arms. Though dry, it felt like an ooze. It wasn't just the usual aroma of body odor or the various and no-doubt-unhealthy construction smells; this was like a weight hanging in the air, like everything was getting ready to fall in and bury me, while I just watched, helpless.

People's "1" pins flashed like holiday lights. No one asked about Moore or Erica. I was getting glares, angry glares, like everyone just knew I'd been involved with that wicked, wicked newspaper, even though the police swore they'd keep me anonymous.

The explanation for that was easy. After all, Moore had been screaming my name. But man, for Cravemen Dylan and Mike to spread it around so brazenly, naming me a witness to the scene of their crime, was downright eerie.

What had happened to this place? At least when we were lame we weren't so damn angry.

The Otus, the newspaper that was supposed to save the day, had gone over like a lead balloon. The Cravers hated it (surprise, surprise), and everyone else either didn't care or was too afraid to say otherwise. Within forty-eight hours, every copy had mysteriously vanished. Near as I could tell, Drik, Mason, and Guy had, too. We'd never swapped numbers, I hadn't seen them at the hospital, and I didn't spot them in school. I hoped they were all taking that mental health week Drik mentioned.

I stuck with the crowd a lot that day, terrified the highly spiritually motivated goon squad would corner me. I even made a point of not drinking any soda or other liquid, so I wouldn't have to use the bathroom.

I did let myself be alone just once. And well, even then, not exactly alone. I was on my way to creative writing when I spotted a familiar green sweater and swaying blond hair ahead of me in the crowd. I didn't call her name, since I figured she'd just keep walking if she heard my voice, but I still felt like I had to talk to her, warn her, for old times' sake or whatever.

As she passed the entrance to the library, I pulled her off to the side. The second she saw my face, she twisted hers in disgust.

"What?" Vicky said.

"Look, it doesn't matter what you think of me. I just want you to know what you're involved in."

She snarled. "You make me sick. You didn't even see anyone's face, but you accused Dylan and Mike, just to get at the Crave."

"How do you know what I told the police?"

"Grace's father is a lieutenant. You think they're not in trouble at home now? They didn't *do* a thing. That was vile, Caleb, really vile. As bad as that paper accusing Ethan."

"It *was* them, Vicky. Who else has been shoving people around who attack your precious club?"

"I know they get a little pushy and we've talked to them about that, but really, don't you get it yet? Moore was attacked because he wanted to be."

Her eyes were washed over with this kind of glassy zombie version of conviction.

"I don't want to debate the nature of the universe. I just want to warn you about Ethan. I'm not guessing about him. I *know* he was involved in what happened to Mr. Eldridge, and I don't mean just by imanifesting. Ethan is dangerous. Really, really dangerous."

She wasn't fazed in the least. "How? How do you *know*?"

"For once, can't you just trust me?"

"What did you ever do to earn that trust, Caleb? You're obviously just jealous and pathetic."

"Vicky, please, could you just at least consider the possibility? You must still have some feelings for me. Don't you remember when we thought the first Crave came true? Wasn't I the one you kissed?"

Her face went blank. Her nose wrinkled, like maybe she was remembering. She took a slow step closer.

"Caleb," she said softly. I could feel heat rising off her sweater as she leaned in and brought her lips close to my ear. Without an inch between us, she whispered, "When I kissed you in the hall, after our first Crave came true? Even then I was thinking of Ethan."

She whirled and walked off.

Whoa.

She was practically gone, but I called after her, "Oh yeah? Sometimes when I kissed you, I was thinking of Lindsay Lohan, but I was too nice to mention it!"

A few kids wearing "1" pins stopped to stare with hate-filled eyes.

And that was the last time I let myself be alone with anyone from the Crave.

On the lighter side, I didn't have any reason to feel guilty about not warning her anymore. I kind of wished, for old times' sake, though, that she'd told me what was going to happen next, since she must have known.

As it was, I spent most of the next period totally unsuspecting, working on an essay in which I imagined being a thirsty flower trying to bloom in the desert. (Mrs. D's idea, not mine.) When the loudspeaker crackled to life, I was relieved to stop writing that crap. Three chimes heralded an announcement from on high, and Dr. Wyatt's somewhat nasal voice whined from the speaker.

He only interrupts class for important news, like nuclear war, so I guessed he was going to announce the completion of the new gym wing. But, no . . .

"This is a difficult time for our school and our community. Many of you have seen or read the recent issue of our school newspaper focusing on one of our after-school clubs and several students involved in that club."

I sat up straight, craned my neck, and strained my ears.

"This is it," I thought. The so-called adults were finally getting involved. Wyatt would shut down the Crave. Ethan, Dylan, and Mike would be arrested. Truth would triumph over lies. Good would whoop evil's ass. But, no . . .

"Following Mr. Eldridge's accident, the paper was left without an adviser. Rather than close it, we'd hoped the students would monitor themselves in a responsible manner. Instead, we were deeply disappointed by the results. Opinions are one thing, and here at Screech Neck, we prize our freedom of speech, but the authors chose to make unsubstantiated allegations that interfered with an ongoing police investigation. This small group has not only opened our school to possible litigation, but their vitriolic writing likely led to the violent attack on their editor, Alden Moore.

"We do not in any way condone that attack. Screech Neck High has zero tolerance for violence, and as soon as the attackers are discovered, if they are students, they will be expelled.

But it's important to remember that insensitive verbal assaults on the beliefs of others are in themselves a form of violence that also will not be tolerated. The staff of the paper has been suspended until further notice. I would ask that everyone, members of the club and otherwise, take a step back and try to show one another patience, in the best tradition of our school."

Three more tones ended the broadcast. I felt like a minivan had parked on my chest. So now I knew what'd happened to Drik, Mason, and Guy. As the rest of the class got back to being thirsty desert flowers, I sat there stunned, mouth open. I think Mrs. Ditellano was about to say something to me, because I heard her clear her throat. But the bell rang.

How could Wyatt do that? Didn't it bother him that the "club" was sweeping over the school like a neo-Nazi movement? Didn't he notice? Didn't he care? He didn't even mention Erica, or the fact that one of the students he'd suspended was in the hospital with his jaw wired shut. Hadn't the police even told him about the security video?

Then I remembered Eldridge telling me Wyatt had his own "1" pin. The bastard was practically one of them.

There was nothing left to stop Ethan—not the police, not the school. No one could do anything. No one wanted to do anything.

As I headed toward the lunchroom, I found myself breathing faster. If I were Drik, I'd probably think I was in the middle of a full-fledged panic attack. Hell, I probably was. I found myself not walking, or running exactly, but pounding my feet into the linoleum. I didn't know if anyone was watching; I didn't care. I was still in a kind of daze, but a nervous rage was building inside of me, years of priding myself on doing nothing crumbling.

I saw a poster for the next Crave and yanked it off the wall.

For some reason, in my head, I saw the spork. It was piercing the french fry, piercing the plate, making a hole in the table beneath it. I could even practically feel that heavy pipe in my hand, the one Joey had offered me, the one I might have been expected to actually use in a less sophisticated time.

I wondered if I could imanifest it right then and there. As I kicked in the door to the cafeteria, feeling that pipe clutched in my hands, one of the poems Erica used to quote came to my mind.

What rough beast slouches towards Bethlehem to be born?

Me.

The lunchroom was loud, but the door, as it hit the wall, was louder.

Everyone turned to look at me. For once, I was glad of it. You could tell at a glance who was in the Crave and who wasn't. The ones who weren't just looked surprised. The ones who were just glared. Ethan, Vicky, Dylan, Mike, Landon, and Grace were all at one table, managing to temper their glaring with a look of righteousness.

I pointed to Ethan. "Skinson! You're a goddamned liar!" I screamed.

He picked his head up, put his hands palm up, and spoke loudly. "What did I lie about, Caleb? Name one thing I've said that isn't true."

I took a few steps forward. "Everything. This used to be a pretty good school before you got here!"

Surprisingly, a few kids clapped—lamely, but they clapped. But then, like a giant snake, a bigger hiss rose from everyone else. Dylan started to get up, but he gritted his teeth and remained seated.

"What was the best part, Dunne?" Ethan said with a grin. "The collapsed side of the school, or the part that kept losing basketball games?"

Unfortunately, he had a point.

"At least we weren't dropping like flies," I shouted, coming closer. "At least our teachers weren't having their brake lines *cut* so people could avoid their tests! And our newspaper editors weren't being attacked by stupid Neanderthals."

Now Dylan did get up. So did Mike. Other kids stood, too, all over the room, forming a big circle that had me and Ethan's table at the center.

Ethan eyed the crowd. "That was *Erica's* Crave. And weren't *you* the one who pushed for it?"

I was busy trying to think of a clever retort when something hit the side of my face. Wet stickiness overwhelmed my right eye. I raised my hand and felt syrupy chunks of apple and crust clinging to my cheek. Someone had thrown a slice of pie at me.

As I was trying to clear my eye, more food filled the air. Some beans. Fries. A wiener. Then people started shoving each other.

"Calm down! Calm down!" Ethan was shouting.

Through blurry vision, I saw a few panicked lunchroom

attendants rush out from the serving area. The hall monitors were coming in through the doors.

I also caught a glimpse of Dylan, headed my way.

Something heavier, maybe a book or a chair, slammed me in the back. I fell forward, slipped on the pie I'd wiped from my face, and the next thing I knew I was eating linoleum. People were going at it, tussling. When the tangled web of limbs parted for a moment, I saw Dylan still trying to get to me, but he couldn't. The crowd was too thick even for him.

But someone else reached me. Two strong hands grabbed the cloth of my overshirt and pulled. I wasn't lifted, but I slid along the floor. Disoriented, I flopped over some feet, then sloshed through a pool of soda and ice, cold bubbles freezing my back.

"Hey!" I shouted, but whoever it was didn't hear me or didn't care. And they were moving fast. The voices of the mob were growing louder, angrier, mixing with the hard clacks of pushed chairs and the wet thuds of hurled food.

It was sounding like a major riot.

I heard doors open and found myself yanked full body onto the relatively clean floor of a dim hallway. As the doors swung shut and the roar inside the cafeteria was muffled, I wound up eyeballing fluorescent ceiling fixtures and a display case showing the sole trophy the Screech Neck Basket Cases had won twenty years ago. Third place. Gaining my bearings, I pivoted awkwardly on my damp shirt and looked up into the face of my rescuer, whose hands were still on me.

Ethan.

"Get off me!" I shouted, twisting away.

He let go and rose, panting slightly. "I saved your ass," Ethan said. "They were going to kill you."

He put a hand out to help me to my feet. On my knees now, I swatted it away.

"I said get off!"

"Suit yourself."

Ethan stepped back as if he were abandoning my lost soul. As soon as I was half standing, I rammed the top of my head into his gut. Together, we sprawled onto the hallway floor. Blood pounded in my ears, mixed with the distant screams of the students and the newer shouts of school officials trying to restore order.

Ethan stood first, legs shoulder-length apart, too perfectly balanced. He waited until I had a chance to stand, then shoved me in the shoulders. When I tried to shove back, he hopped out of the way, leaving me stumbling.

"Will you knock it off? Someone could see us," Ethan said. "What is it with you, anyway? Is this about Vicky?"

"No," I said. "You tried to kill Mr. Eldridge."

He blinked. For half a second, he looked afraid, but then that calm, steely mask that made him look like he was thirty slipped back over his features. "If you insist on thinking in that backward way, then so did you, every time you imanifested everyone passing the algebra test."

"Bullshit," I said. "You cut his brake line."

I pulled back and took a swing at him, but my eye was still tearing from the cinnamon and sugar, so he ducked easily.

"You *really* don't want to fight me, Dunne," Ethan said.

"Yeah, I do," I said.

He chuckled like a super-villain. "Okay, fine, but let's try to be a little smarter about it, okay? Not now, not here. That way, no suspensions."

I panted. "Okay. Name the time and place."

"Saturday night, midnight. In the new gym."

I blinked and wiped my eye again. "What?"

He was so calm, so sure of himself. My own, unreliable rage was already fading, the image of the spork, or the pipe clenched in my hand, disintegrating.

"That's right. You and me, once and for all, in the new gym. You know the place, don't you? After all, you helped create it."

He must have been imanifesting for me to agree, because even though I knew it was the stupidest thing I'd ever done, I said yes.

The next day it was as if an eerie truce had descended between me and the Cravers. I even walked by Dylan a few times, and he didn't so much as snarl. Maybe it was because Wyatt came down so hard on everyone involved in the cafeteria "food fight"—thirty people got detention—or maybe it was because I accepted Ethan's challenge and word was out that I should be left alone until Saturday.

I don't know what I was thinking when I said yes to that fight.

Well, yeah, I do. I was thinking it'd be really sweet to punch him a couple of times, slam him around a bit, and make him hurt. More interesting are all the things I *wasn't* thinking—how if I got caught, with Wyatt still considering me responsible for the building collapse, I'd be totally, permanently expelled. I also wasn't thinking that, as a slacker, if I could even still consider myself one, I didn't believe in violence. Nor had I truly considered that even if I won, other than making me feel better for a little while, what good would it do? Ethan would just give everyone some variation of his "I really meant for that to happen" speech, and everyone would slap Mr. Psycho on the back.

I went to visit Erica at the hospital again that afternoon, but I sure didn't want to talk to her about school. The overdose had left her with some kind of stomach ulcer that was aggravated by anxiety. She was having enough trouble recuperating without hearing that I was about to battle to the death. So I was all smiles, talking favorite TV shows and movies while she talked novels and poetry. I thought I'd pulled it off quite nicely until she grabbed my hand and said, "What's wrong?"

"What?"

"Something's been bothering you since you got here. What is it? The Crave after you?"

"What? No. I'm fine. I'm, uh . . . just going to go see Moore now. You take care."

She knew it was an excuse. I knew she knew, but I wasn't going to talk. I already felt like I'd failed her the first time, by not telling someone about her notebook. I didn't want to fail her again. I was surprised by how strongly I felt about her lately, and this time it wasn't the cookies.

To date my visits with Moore hadn't been fun for either of us with his jaw wired shut. Unable to exercise his gift for being verbally annoying, he mostly just lay there watching TV. I figured I'd drop in and bring him some soda from the vending machines. Quick in and out, in case Erica was watching.

But as I neared his room, I heard familiar voices.

"In a couple of days those wires will be gone, and you won't be able to shut up."

"I TiVo'd this week's *Lost* episode for you. I'll burn you a DVD."

"And don't worry about Saturday—we've got it fixed so we can all watch the fight together."

Seconds later, Mason, Drik, and Guy stepped out into the hall. Their clothing was unusually sedate, T-shirts, coats, and jeans all around, as if they were traveling incognito. I was thrilled to see them.

"Hey! What the hell have you all been up to?" I said. "Couldn't you have given me a call or sent an e-mail or . . . something?"

"Sorry, Dunne, this was the first time we even had a chance to visit Moore," Guy said.

"You've been *suspended*. You've got nothing but time."

"We can't all run around accepting challenges from Ethan," Mason said. "Think they'll give you a room next to Alden?"

I furrowed my brow. "I suppose by now I shouldn't be surprised by what you know. Is it up on the Crave message board?"

Guy waved off the thought. "We got blocked out. They changed passwords."

"We did find out that the police *were* showing Eldridge's security video around all along, only they were doing it quietly, with local residents and a few students. No one was able to identify the attacker," Mason said.

"Another dead end," I sighed. "Unless I lie and say I *was* there."

"Don't bother. You'd never pass the poly. However . . . ,"

Drik said. He looked mysteriously up and around. "We have been doing something a little more proactive . . ."

"Drik . . . ," Mason warned.

"He should know," Drik said. "He's practically one of us."

"Know what?" I asked. "Come on! I went through a whole police interrogation, and I didn't squeal."

Guy sidled up to me and lowered his voice even more. "Okay. Want to come over to my house tonight for a few hours? Around eight?"

There are no ritzy sections of Screech Neck. During economic boom times, when you couldn't help but make money, there were a few upscale developments planned. Concrete foundations were even poured, but not a single McMansion was ever completed, leaving Screech Neck pretty much all old and drab. There were apartment buildings near the center of town, where I lived, and 1960s single- and two-family houses at the outskirts of town, where Ethan and his family lived, but there was also a kind of dreary sameness to it all.

On the one hand, you never felt like you were in a particularly bad neighborhood, but on the other, you never felt totally safe. That's a roundabout way of saying that Davis Street, where Guy lived, was pretty nondescript, a row of two-family houses lining the street, so close to each other that if you opened a side window, you could reach into your neighbor's kitchen to borrow the mustard.

Once I reached the address, it took me a second of staring at the names beside the door to realize Guy's family lived in the basement. A little arrow pointed down some cracked stone steps where I found a small white buzzer. After I pressed it, a light came on inside, the door creaked open, and I was greeted by a short woman in a housecoat. Her hair was up in curlers. A lit cigarette dangled from her mouth.

I cleared my throat. "Guy here?"

"*Guy!*" she howled. I was impressed the cigarette didn't fall.

His voice called from inside. "Send him back, Mom!"

The dangler stepped out of my way and I entered. There was only one light on in the living room, a small lamp with maybe a twenty-watt bulb in it. Looking down, I realized I was standing on old newspapers, which seemed to cover most of the floor. The ceiling was low, and even though there wasn't much furniture, it felt crowded.

The creak of the door closing behind me made me whirl.

The dangler was gone.

"Guy?" I called out.

"Here," he said.

I felt my way through the dimness to a door at the end of a hall. When I pushed it open, a dull green-blue glow met my eyes.

Inside were Guy, Drik, and Mason, all in chairs facing the source of the glow, a monitor. It was an old tube-type, big, maybe twenty-one inches, with speakers on either side, hooked by a few wires to Guy's laptop. Between the chairs, tables of snack food were laid out. No one acknowledged me. They were all busy munching and staring at the screen.

"Think she'll do it?" Guy said to Mason.

Mason shook her head. "Nah. See how fed up she is?"

Last time they'd showed me a monitor, I'd been shocked by what I saw. This time it was just the same. On it was a blocky webcam image, blown up way too big for the screen. The frame rate was low, the movement jerky. If it was in color, I couldn't tell. There were two figures on it, a male standing in the center of the frame, arms out, like he was pleading, and a shorter girl, some papers in her hand, with her arms crossed, like she was saying no. The angle was off, the way you'd see in some hidden-camera TV show. Then I realized why.

It was Ethan and Alyssa.

That familiar dulcet voice came through the tinny speakers, tinged with impatience. "Just one picture, Alyssa. Just one drawing of me beating him. Please."

"Holy crap!" I shouted. "You put a *webcam* in Ethan's room!? How did you—"

"Shh!" they all said.

"That's breaking and entering! And . . . and . . . wiretapping! Do you know how many laws you're—"

"Shh!" they said again.

Mason pointed to a chair next to her. Amazed, I sat.

On screen, Alyssa was yelling at Ethan, shaking her head.

"Come on, Ethan, this is just because my pictures remind you of Mom! What are you going to ask for next? You think I can bring her back from the dead?"

"Maybe."

She was genuinely upset. "I can't do it anymore anyway, even if I wanted!"

He stiffened. "What do you mean?"

Guy leaned forward and whispered, "We've been waiting for him to confess about cutting the brake lines, but so far, nothing."

"Shh!" Mason said again.

"It never worked the way you said to begin with, and now it doesn't work at all. I can't even draw a decent picture."

"It can't just stop working. It's a natural law of the universe."

"Then maybe you should get a lawyer," she said.

Alyssa held up the papers in her hand, crinkling them as she thrust them toward Ethan. "I've been drawing for six days, and not one picture has happened. Not one."

He took them, looked at the pile, and unfolded one or two carefully, like they were holy relics. He shook his head as Alyssa continued to speak.

"Maybe my battery wore out, okay? Or maybe I broke something or maybe it was like I've been saying all along, *just a bunch of coincidences to begin with!*"

He put the papers down on his desk and shook his head furiously. "No, no, no! It's not! There's no such thing as coincidence! Do you understand? No such thing!"

She snarled back in a voice that again reminded me whose sister she was. "Then maybe you're being punished for being too greedy!"

He slammed his hands down on the desk. "This was your last chance, Alyssa. Your talent was a gift from Mom, but you betrayed it. Your drawings don't work anymore because you've let negativity creep into your mind. I don't have that negativity. Not one ounce."

He went on like that for a while. By the time Ethan finally stopped, Alyssa was shivering. Not from cold. More like she was going to really just let loose and scream at him. She must've thought better of it, though, because she ran out.

He closed the door behind her, then stood alone in the center of his room, inhaling slow and steady. His arms curved in time with his deep breathing, rolling out into the air, then back toward his body.

"What's all that about?" Mason asked.

"He's calming himself down," Drik offered.

"It's yogic," Guy said. "Look at his control. Dunne, you should take notes for the fight."

Right. Notes on how best to lose. Ethan repeated the motion, faster and faster, until his fists were snapping into the air. I could hear little popping noises, like he was punching air molecules. Then he bobbed on the balls of his feet and added some quick kicks, his heel reaching over his head.

"Kung fu?"

"It's some kind of martial art."

My eyes got wide. "Holy crap," I said.

Until then, I was thinking I at least had a shot at beating Ethan. He was a little bigger than me, but not much more muscular, and I figured I had rage on my side. Plus, he was so arrogant, he was easy to surprise. I thought if I took him down quickly, it could all be over in a minute.

But as I watched him kick, punch, and twist in the air like a video game character, it dawned on me that imanifestations were the least of my worries. Even without the collected wishes of the club, odds were damn good that the son of a bitch was going to cream me.

"Holy crap," I repeated.

Someone handed me a bottle of soda. I poured it over my head, let the cola drip down my face and sting my eyes. Maybe I was hoping it would wake me up from the nightmare, but it didn't.

Finally, Ethan shut the light in his room to go to sleep. Guy flicked the monitor off and said, "You're utterly doomed."

Mason turned to me. "Still going?"

I shrugged. "If I don't, they'll get me like they got Moore. At least you guys can be there to scrape me off the floor."

"Oh, *we're* not going," Drik said.

"What?"

Mason shook her head. "Too dangerous. They all want to kill us."

"And this is different from my situation how?"

"We will be there in spirit," Guy offered. "I planted another webcam in the gym. We're going to break into the hospital and watch on my laptop with Moore."

I stared at them, unbelieving.

"Sorry, dude," Drik said. "But, hey, if it looks like you're really dying or something, we'll call the cops."

Guy patted me sympathetically on the shoulder. "Want another soda to pour over your head? There's two left in the fridge."

I had nothing to say to that. I had nothing left to say. In fact, the next day, the day before the fight, I was real quiet, developing the kind of darkly fatal attitude that would have made Erica proud—if I'd told her about it.

It got worse around midday. Much worse. I was walking along the hall to my locker when my foot found a sheet of paper on the floor. There was some kind of drawing on it, so I picked it up for a closer look. The art wasn't Alyssa's, but you could still make out that it was me and Ethan. Ethan was holding me up by my neck as blood streamed out of my eyes. Apparently the Cravers were branching out into their own adventures in drawing. Chanting was no longer enough. Or maybe Ethan was hedging his bets, trying to find an artist to replace Alyssa.

I crumpled it up and tossed it out. When I opened my locker, though, a ton more tumbled out: loose-leaf sheets, pages torn from pads, matchbook covers, you name it. Each had a drawing, some with pencil stick figures, some full bodied. The Cravers were also diverse in their choice of medium—pencil, charcoal, watercolor, even oils. There wasn't much variation in their subject, though. All of them showed Ethan triumphant and me lying dead, or near to it.

At least I didn't have to wonder what they'd decided this week's Crave was going to be.

I thought about showing the collection to Dr. Wyatt or the cops, but none were signed, and what would it change? I shoved them back in, closed the locker, and headed to class.

On the way, I heard some steady whispering. As it got louder, I slowed down and stayed near the wall. Edging around the corner, I saw about ten kids in a huddle, kids I didn't even know, all chanting, fast and low:

Ethan will beat Caleb Dunne.

Ethan will beat Caleb Dunne.

Ethan will beat Caleb Dunne.

I didn't interrupt them, I just backed slowly away, found the nearest door, and cut the rest of the day. Funny, I'd been thinking I should stay as long as I could, especially since this might be my last day at Screech Neck High, if I got caught at the fight, but as I sat on the bus watching the scaffolding that surrounded the new gym wing vanish among the buildings and trees, I was just happy to get away.

Sitting in the back where the smell of the exhaust was nice and strong, I closed my eyes and banged the back of my head against the window. I was thinking of calling upon my spork and trying to imanifest myself winning. Why not? Ethan and the book never talked about what would happen if people had opposing imanifestations.

Would whoever wished hardest win, or was it more like a lot of little wishing added up to one great big wish? Or would the world split into two dimensions, one where I was triumphant and sanity was restored to Screech Neck, the other where I lay dead and everyone was forced to wear "1" pins by law?

A little dose of reality snapped me out of that. The bus window I was leaning against doubled as an emergency exit. It must have been broken or at least loose, because when I pushed back harder, it swung open at the bottom, sending a blast of November chill into my hair. You get a nice cold blast of air on the back of your head like that, and really, all you can think of is how cold your head is.

I appreciated the distraction. By the time I got home, I was realizing how totally stupid and insane I was for even thinking about showing up. I was a slacker, right? I could just not go. I could run away to another state and start over as a retail clerk.

Joey, at the dining room table, raised his weathered head as I came in. "Cutting class?"

"No. I just feel kind of sick."

I must have looked so miserable, he didn't bother to challenge me on it. "Take a hot shower or something. That'll perk you up."

"Sure."

"Oh," he added in that gravelly voice of his. "Package came for you."

He pushed a small box, wrapped in brown paper, across the table. My name was written on it in pen.

"Buy something on eBay?"

"With what?" I smirked at him as I fumbled with the wrapping.

The paper was held on with two small strips of Scotch tape. I was surprised it had held together this long, because it just came apart in my hands, revealing a worn sleeve. It was pocked with white where the ink had rubbed away, but you could still make out the title, *Mondo Cane*.

"Hey, Joey," I said. "Can I borrow your VHS player?"

- I see him just collapsing, eyes rolling into the back of his head. I picture Ethan punching him, over and over, bruising, then breaking the skin. I don't picture Caleb Dunne dead, but he's really wishing he was. —Colleen

- I give my power to Ethan. I put my strength in his arms, behind his blows. I imagine myself slamming my clenched fist into Caleb Dunne's face, feeling his nose collapse under my fingers. I see Ethan tower over him, only he's not just Ethan, he's all of us. We are part of it and part of everything. —Mike

- Caleb Dunne is so going to get his ass totally kicked by Ethan, and when he's finished, I'm next in line. —Dylan

- The marines have taught my brother sixteen ways to kill a man with his hands. I picture Ethan using them all on Dunne. —Alex

- According to the book, it's okay to remove obstacles, but we really shouldn't ever wish ill will on people. So we have to make sure we don't think of Caleb Dunne as a person. He's not really. He's made himself an obstacle, a thing that stands in the way of spreading the truth. So it's perfectly okay that he should lose and suffer for it. —Grace

- I see Caleb Dunne getting whacked, over and over, with Nicole's iPhone, until they both just . . . break. —Sophia

- I've got some kind of freaky blood disease. The doctor thinks it's because I somehow wore down my immune system, but I know the real explanation: Caleb Dunne and his downer thoughts. He's what made me sick, so I'm devoting all my energies, all my imanifesting, to turning that negativity back on him, to give him the blurry vision, to give him the headaches and the crappy parents who want to send me to some detox camp, to give him the pain he wants to give everyone else. —Jane

- I hope at the last minute Caleb Dunne realizes what a fool he's been, that he sees the light, that he comes back to us with his head down and his heart open. —Jacob

- Anyone who tries to destroy us deserves whatever they get. No pity for Caleb Dunne. He tried to hurt my family and now he's going to see just how strong and together we all are. —Olivia

- I would like the new Xbox 360 Elite System, with a premium black finish and three powerful core processors capable of producing the best in HD entertainment (up to 1080p, like any Xbox 360), 16:9 cinematic aspect ratio, anti-aliasing for smooth textures, full surround sound, HDMI output, and DVD playback with upscaling capabilities right out of the box. I would also like to see Ethan kick Caleb's ass. —Landon

- I don't know if I can make it to the fight, but I'll be there with you in spirit, imanifesting so hard, you'll probably actually see me there! Go, Ethan! Down with Caleb Dunne! —Andrew

- I'm worried about some of you. I'm still thinking there are dark thoughts out there, maybe even some we're not aware of, like people afraid to show up because the cops might come. We'll see who's there and who's not. We'll see. —Jeff

- I picture a warm white glow surrounding all of us with health and power. I picture a golden shield nothing can penetrate, not knives, not bullets, not hate. I picture it growing, swelling out and around us, taking in more and more of the world, welcoming in all the riches, and pushing out all the stalkers and all the Caleb Dunnes. —Kathleen

- I guess I don't see the connection between Caleb Dunne and global warming. Is he really that important? Shouldn't we just ignore him? —Beth

- Everyone's watching this, everyone. I was talking to one of the members in the hall the other day about the fight and the PE teacher Mr. Canner was listening in. I was terrified he was going to turn us in, but he just winked and showed me the "1" pin he wears under his jacket. We cannot be defeated. —Tom

- It's like everything I've been afraid of is finally coming to a head. It's going to end on Saturday, all of it, I just know it is. It's going to end with this fight, and then I am going to be free. —Lauren

- I see Caleb lying on the ground, pleading, crying, begging me to help him, showing more true emotion than I've ever seen from him, more than I even thought he was capable of. And then I tell him, This is what you wanted and now you've got it—you've got it all. —Vicky

I'd really, truly been hoping *Mondo Cane* would provide some sort of *Rule*-like secret that'd allow me to defeat Ethan and the Crave.

Nope.

Turns out, it was pretty lame. It was this old documentary from the sixties. Most of it was stuff I guess at the time they considered gross and shocking—people eating dog meat and insects and stuff. There were some sick violent rituals, too, like animal sacrifices. There was also this really long sequence of cars being crushed, which didn't seem to have much to do with anything.

And yeah, at long last, there was the Vanuatu. Finally. Vanuatu's an island nation in the South Pacific and the home of what's called a cargo cult, which basically worships cargo. During World War II there was an air base there and the locals, who weren't technologically advanced (and when I say that, I mean they had spears and clothes and agriculture and that was about it), developed a sort of religion around what they saw at the air base. They came to believe that the giant metal birds and all the stuff they carried was really meant for them, that the white men who'd built the airport had tricked the gods into bringing the cargo to the wrong people.

So, to get the goodies of the gods back, they built fake airports, fake control towers, even fake airplanes, all out of bamboo and wood. Some of them even made fake soldier uniforms for themselves. Then they'd sit around, manning the fake airport, tending the fake planes, hoping a real one would show up and give them stuff.

What any of this had to do with *The Rule of Won* was beyond me. It did provide a last distraction before my rendezvous with destiny—also known as waiting-to-get-the-crap-kicked-out-of-me-by-some-psycho-who'd-studied-martial-arts-all-his-life-and-didn't-think-much-of-cutting-people's-brake-lines.

The whole running-away thing sounded like the only sane choice. Screech Neck had never been great to me, so what was I hanging around for? By Saturday night at ten, with Joey snoring on the couch, I was packed and ready to go.

But then the lock in the door rattled and in walked my mom, carrying so many grocery bags she practically fell into the apartment.

"Some help, Caleb?" she said.

I stumbled up and helped her unpack, feeling like a heel that she even had to ask.

"Long time no see," I said. I meant it as a joke, but I could tell it made her feel guilty.

"I'm trying to change my schedule, honey, but the new manager's got something to prove, so he's not even listening," she said with a yawn.

"Tell him to screw off," I told her.

I always wished she had a little more slacker in her. But apparently I got all that from my dad, the one who ran off when I was three. The one whose face I didn't even remember.

"Wish I could, but the homeless shelter's a little cramped this time of year. How are things at school since that poor boy got attacked? And what are you doing home early on a Saturday? Aren't you still seeing that nice girl Vicky?"

I wanted to say, "Nope. Turns out she's Satan and she's dating this guy who tried to kill a teacher and wants to beat me up tonight."

But Mom's eyes were half closed, so I sort of shrugged. "We split up a while ago."

She patted me on the shoulder. "Oh, I'm sorry. It'll work out."

"Yeah," I said.

She twisted her head, looked me in the eyes, and rubbed my temples with her thumbs, like she could squeeze the worry in my face away. "Are you all right?"

"Sure. Fine."

She scanned me, trying to read the truth in my face. "No, you're not, but you're not going to tell me about it, are you?"

"Mom . . ."

"I'm sorry, Caleb. I used to be so sure things would be different. I was so sure your father would come back, so sure I'd have a better job, so sure we'd move out of Screech Neck, so sure at least I'd be able to see you more, but all of it just never happened, and here you are, almost grown."

Her eyes watered a bit, so I hugged her.

"It's okay, Mom. You're doing great. I'm fine. Really. I love you."

You know, even if everything else hadn't already convinced me *The Rule* was a crock, that sure did. She wanted all that stuff for me, pictured it so perfectly, but she got none of it.

She sniffed and nodded, and we went back to her unpacking. Fifteen minutes later, she was in her bedroom, asleep, and I was realizing I couldn't run away and leave her and Joey behind.

Just couldn't.

Which left me pondering the best of the worst-case scenarios. At least if I showed, and Ethan beat me up a bit, everyone might be satisfied and just leave me alone. Dylan and his pals, after all, did things like break jaws. Maybe Ethan would be more merciful.

Satisfied I was the only one left in the apartment who wasn't dreaming, I put on a peacoat, an old hand-me-down from Joey. I always thought that was the most ridiculous name ever for a piece of clothing (What do you wear with it? Carrot-pants?), but it was warm.

And I slipped out the door.

It was cold enough for the crisp air to sting my face and for my breath to hang like a little cloud in front of me whenever I exhaled. When the bus didn't show on time, I jogged toward school to warm up. About two stops down the line, I heard the vacuum-cleaner roar of the bus engine and waited for it to catch up.

It was empty except for me and a grouchy driver who seemed annoyed he had to open the door for me. After I paid my fare, I found a warm seat near the back and let the chill slip out of my bones. I thought about my spork, about imanifesting a winning night for myself, or at least one where I survived, but I decided not to. Win or lose, I was going to do this without *The Rule,* finally prove to myself beyond any doubt whether it really worked or not.

Twenty minutes later, I was at SNH standing on the same small hill overlooking the construction that I'd been on in January. With the work almost finished, it was looking pretty much the same as it had then. Apparently they hadn't bothered to redesign it or use different material.

Funny, if I hadn't been here last winter and run, Alden Moore never would have seen me. I never would have been suspended, never would have joined the Crave. Of course Vicky and I probably would still have broken up, and the Crave would still have happened in all its weird glory, but at least I wouldn't have been so tied up in it.

Or would I? I might have gotten to know Erica anyway, then seen that book of hers and gotten worried just the same. But would I have gotten involved or just stayed a slacker, minding my own business, just watching things collapse?

If a school building falls and no one's there to hear it, does it make a sound?

Time to go in.

The new gym, like the old, like any school gym, I guess, has tall windows. Through them I could see light inside, a white glow that didn't even reach the top of those windows, instead petering out in a semicircle about halfway up.

As I made my way to the entrance, I heard the low sound of many voices. They were all chanting, of course (say it with me, now):

Ethan will beat Caleb Dunne.

Ethan will beat Caleb Dunne.

Ethan will beat Caleb Dunne.

The door, as promised, was wedged open. Taking in the mother of all deep breaths, I pushed it and walked inside.

To borrow a phrase, OMG.

Most every kid from SNH must have been there, at least the whole Crave. Each head swayed back and forth as they chanted. Lit flashlights stood in regular spots on the floor, sending columns of dusty white light into the air, accounting for the windows' dull glow. Looking like a herd of wildebeests, they stood, sat, and leaned, but all faced the same way, toward the same far wall.

It was the only wall that remained unfinished. Two scaffolds stood against the cinder-block construction, a wide space between them, like they were the light rig for a rock show. On the shiny new floor in front of it, a large white circle had been painted with the number "1" in the center.

In the middle of that circle stood Ethan.

He wore a black martial arts outfit. His fists were clenched and facing each other. His head was bent, but I could see his lips moving. He had his sneakers on, their bleached white laces glowing almost as brightly as the flashlight beams.

Ethan will beat Caleb Dunne. Ethan will beat Caleb Dunne.

It was like walking into some kind of freaking zombie ritual.

I had a hard time trying to get through the mob to reach the circle. No one moved out of my way until (thankfully?) Dylan spotted me, and he and Mike cleared a path for their sacrificial lamb.

I noticed a ball of duct tape stuck to the edge of one of the scaffolds like a bird's nest. Figuring that must be Guy's web-cam, I gave it a wave and a smile.

"What do *you* have to grin about?" Dylan asked.

I looked him dead in the eyes. "Because I'm going to kick your master's ass, dog-boy."

Hey, if you're on a roller coaster to hell, you might as well stick your arms up and scream, right?

Dylan was ready to pound me into a beef patty right there, but Mike pulled me ahead and shoved me into the circle with Ethan.

As I crossed the white line, I took a bit of the paint up with my foot. It was some kind of watercolor thing that they could clean up easily enough. At least they were considerate crazy people. Or maybe they just didn't want to leave any evidence.

The moment I entered, the chanting stopped. Just stopped, like a switch had been flipped. I looked at all the staring faces. Many of these friends and strangers, just a week before, had been slapping me on the back like I was their best buddy.

One figure stood out, a slight girl, hair hidden by the cloth of a hoodie, face concealed by wide sunglasses. Despite the threat of the coming beating, I said to myself, "Geez, who'd wear sunglasses in a gym lit by flashlights at night?"

But when she cried out, "Get him, Ethan!" and everyone howled, I knew who. It was Vicky, trying to remain incognito because of her growing political career. Wouldn't want to be recognized here if the police showed up, right? It might look bad on her record.

Ethan raised his hands to quiet everyone.

Not bothering to look at me, he called out, "Landon here?"

The former Goth lumbered out from the mass to the circle's edge. He hesitated at the white line, but Ethan nodded him in.

As Landon came forward, Ethan picked up a box he'd been standing in front of and held it out. He said, not shouting, but loud enough for everyone to hear, "The universe is one of eternal abundance. Take what is yours."

And he handed Landon the box.

Landon's eyes got nearly as big as his head as he realized what it was: an Xbox 360. The big guy shook, he was so happy. The damn thing had been so important to him, I felt good for him, too, until he shouted maniacally, "Ethan will beat Caleb Dunne!"

Everyone howled again as Landon held the box over his head and ran through the crowd, cheering wildly.

Okay, so maybe it was more like a game show than a zombie ritual.

Finally, Ethan turned to me. "It's simple. First one who leaves or gets thrown out of the circle loses. Got it?"

"Yeah," I said. I shook my arms and stretched my neck, trying to look like I knew what I was doing.

Ethan bent over and undid the laces of his sneakers. Head down, he whispered so I could hear: "I'll give you one chance to just walk out of the circle on your own now. Do it and I'll tell everyone to leave you alone."

I eyed the circle, I eyed the crowd. Would they let me go if Ethan said so? Maybe. I'll never know what I would have decided. Ethan was lying anyway.

Next thing I knew, his foot slammed into my mouth. It didn't even feel like a foot, unless it was a foot strapped to the front of a pickup truck doing about sixty. I have no idea what Moore felt like when his jaw broke, but I'm guessing this was close.

My head snapped back. My body followed a full second later, like it had finally gotten around to wondering where my head had gone off to. To keep from falling backward and cracking my skull, I lobbed myself forward onto my knees.

That's where the side of my face met his other foot.

I may have gone unconscious for a second or so. My ears rang. My skull throbbed. No, it wasn't a throbbing. It was that damn chant.

Ethan will beat Caleb Dunne. Ethan will beat Caleb Dunne.

Somehow, I stood. I made out something blurry that

looked like Ethan. Not wanting to go down without some sort of fight, I ran for him, shoving my head into his gut. It was like hitting a wall.

He didn't look built out of muscle like Dylan. Maybe his martial arts training let him turn his body into a solid piece of mahogany, or maybe he really was absorbing some kind of unnatural strength from the crowd.

Ethan will beat Caleb Dunne. Ethan will beat Caleb Dunne.

Didn't matter much, y'know? He grabbed my head and pulled me toward the edge of the circle. Maybe six feet from it he grunted, twisted, and hurled. I went flying. This was it. No way could I stop myself from hurtling out. It'd all be over in a flash. I felt good about that, actually, what with still being alive and all.

But it was just another of Ethan's tricks. Before I could sail out of the circle and end the match, he grabbed my right hand and pulled me back in, nearly yanking my arm out of its socket.

I sprawled to the ground in front of him.

Aside from being tremendously painful, it was ridiculous. He could win any time he wanted. He just wanted to make the part where he beat the piss out of me last as long as possible.

Ethan will beat Caleb Dunne. Ethan will beat Caleb Dunne.

Once I realized that, I had a new goal—get the hell out of the circle. Agreeing with this strategy, an animal survival instinct kicked in and gave me a burst of energy. I stood—well, half stood, anyway—and ran for it. As soon as they figured out what I was trying to do, everyone booed.

Tough crowd.

I thought I was going to make it, but I felt a fist in my gut and tumbled over from pain. Ethan dragged me to the center of the circle, my body smudging the white paint of the giant "1." Things were dim, but it looked like the white paint was speckled with red. Blood. Mine. The crowd cheered, happy again.

Ethan leaned over me and whispered, "What made you think you could go against *The Rule*? Against me?"

My voice was hoarse. One of my teeth felt loose. "Kind of had to, Ethan. You tried to kill Mr. Eldridge."

He brought his head closer to my ear. "I had doubts, too, Caleb, when I cut that brake line. Then I realized I wasn't just acting for myself. I was part of something much, much bigger. I'd become a tool of *The Rule*. A tool of the universe."

"You're a tool all right," I said. "A real tool."

Sometimes I just don't know when to keep my mouth closed.

Ethan shut it for me, letting loose a flurry of punches on my face and chest. I slumped like a sack of potatoes. Bruised and bleeding potatoes.

My fellow students went wild with pleasure.

Ethan will beat Caleb Dunne! Ethan will beat Caleb Dunne!

"Get up," Ethan said.

I couldn't. He took my arm and pulled me up.

I could open only one eye, but through it, I saw him point at the circle's edge.

"Walk out. Now."

Ethan will beat Caleb Dunne! Ethan will beat Caleb Dunne!

I hoped he meant it this time, because it sounded awfully good to me. I didn't want to walk out into the crowd, though. They didn't seem to like me. I staggered toward the edge of the circle that faced the wall, the one with the two scaffolds.

Ethan will beat Caleb Dunne! Ethan will beat Caleb Dunne!

As I got closer to the edge, I could feel everyone ready to break into cheers. What would happen after that? Maybe they'd let me make it to the door, maybe they wouldn't. Maybe I'd only been stupid enough to show up here because part of me wanted this all to happen, because part of me wanted to be punished for daring to challenge Ethan Skinson and *The Rule*.

My bad.

I got closer to the edge, hoping Mason, Drik, and Guy would remember their promise to call an ambulance. Every step was agony. About a foot from the white paint, I glanced up into the webcam. I stopped a second and tried to breathe. When I inhaled, there was a sharp pain in my side, like a rib had been broken. When I exhaled, I made a gurgling noise.

Then, for some reason I'll never, ever get, or maybe for some wild, brazen *lack* of reason, I turned, faced Ethan with my one eye, and said, "No."

He didn't seem surprised. "Suit yourself."

He took a few lightning-quick steps to cover the distance between us.

As I watched him, my mind went blank, not in terror or anything, but in a totally calm way. It was like for a single, shining moment, I didn't picture *anything* at all, like all this time I'd really only been pretending to have an empty open mind, and this, out of nowhere and from nowhere, was the real deal. No spork. No nothing.

It was the Ultimate Slacker Moment.

For that second, I really didn't want anything. I didn't want to escape. I didn't want not to escape. I didn't want to lose (no-brainer there), but I also didn't want to win. I was just there. The world was just there, and there we were, together.

I heard the chanting crowd like it was in slow motion. I heard Ethan's heavy breathing, smelled his sweat. I even heard the slight rush of air as he launched his body into the air for his perfectly placed final kick. His foot came up toward my face with what looked like enough force to send me through the wall. Then . . .

I floated.

Actually, I just dropped, gently and completely and totally out of the way.

Ethan's foot hit air. His eyes were just beginning to widen when his body found itself pulled forward by the force of his own kick. He went past me—out of the circle, where his heel hit right in the center of that unfinished wall. A few chunks of cinder block and dust flew from the point of impact.

It could have been my skull.

When everybody saw that, instead of erupting into a cheer, the crowd went, "Urgh!" figuring Ethan had broken his foot.

I realized what it meant before he did, so through my one open eye I could watch the realization dawn on his face.

I'd won.

At first he looked surprised, then angry, then shocked, then just . . . lost.

No one said another word. The echo of their last chant died against the walls. The only thing I could hear was breathing—my own.

That is, until a few bits of plaster trickled from the wall and the ceiling. Some tumbled into Ethan's open mouth, making him grimace and spit. When the flow didn't stop and a loud creaking noise, like a giant door opening on giant rusty hinges, began, I looked up at the wall.

The first thing that came to mind was the phrase "Uh-oh."

I got to my feet and backed away.

"Ethan," I said. "Get out of there. The wall's coming down."

Smug and defiant as ever, he shook his head. "No," he said. He turned to the crowd. "We can *stop* it. We can imanifest and stop it!"

You have to remember that all these people had just seen how well their imanifesting worked on the outcome of the big fight between me and Ethan, which, let's face it, was as close to a sure thing as you can get. Now, as Ethan stood in front of a really big pile of trembling cinder block, wood, and concrete, they looked collectively dubious.

Me, I kept backing slowly away.

"Come on!" Ethan commanded. He turned to the wall, a huge grin on his face. "This wall will not fall! This wall will not fall!" He turned back to the crowd. "Everyone! Concentrate! This wall will not fall!"

Landon, who owed this man his Xbox 360, after all, stepped up and chanted with him. Now it was the two of them crying out, "This wall will not fall!"

When no one else stepped up and the plaster from the collapsing drywall started to rain harder, Ethan again faced the crowd. "Vicky! Come on!"

She looked around for a moment, pretending not to know who he was speaking to, then with a sigh walked up and stood by her man.

Now it was the three of them versus gravity. "This wall will not fall! This wall will not fall!"

Everyone was so busy looking at them, I made it to the door. Dylan stood there, half blocking my exit. All he had to do was breathe on me to stop me. Instead, he hesitated only a second, gave me a bewildered look, then stepped aside.

I went out into the Screech Neck night, the frigid air stinging my each and every wound. I had enough left in me to climb back up that little hill and watch. I remember wishing, not very hard, but wishing nonetheless, that I had someone to share it with.

That's when a black-haired girl came running up out of the darkness. She was wearing Guy's leather jacket over a hospital gown. Her feet were in slippers.

"Erica?" I said hoarsely.

She sputtered as she raced toward me. "They had the fight on in Moore's room. I thought it was just some stupid YouTube clip. As soon as I realized it was live . . . Caleb, my God! What happened?"

"Uh . . . I won?"

She stood beside me, looking like she wanted to hug me but afraid it would hurt me too much. "That's winning? Are you crazy?"

I managed to shrug. "Sure. A little. You?"

"Yeah. A little."

A louder creaking turned us both back toward the gym. Erica took a step closer and leaned into me. I put an arm around her and we warmed each other up as words floated up from the gym.

"This wall will not fall. This wall will not fall."

Erica couldn't believe it. "Are they chanting?"

"Yeah. Ethan's holding up the school."

The creaking turned into the loud moan of inanimate materials stretched to breaking.

"Or not."

"I called the police," she said. "They'll be here soon."

I squeezed her shoulder a little. "Good," I said. "Let's watch."

We stood there, my arm around her, until a small section of roof wobbled and fell inward. We heard the dulcet voice of Ethan crack as he screamed, "Oh, crap!"

And the chanting stopped.

Ethan was the first out the door, leading a swarm of people into the night. The place was empty by the time the police arrived, the white circle buried in rubble, the new bleachers open to the starry sky.

I later heard that when the gym collapsed and the webcam

went dead, Moore, his jaw newly unwired, shook his head and said, "Vanuatu."

Either out of a newfound respect, embarrassment, or fear of being arrested themselves, no one ratted me out about the fight.

In fact, no one who was there ever spoke about it again.

Moore, whom I've counted as a friend ever since he finally published that article about the flaws in the gym, tells me that in 2007, in Katmandu, Nepal, the state-run airline sacrificed two goats to the Hindu sky god, Akash Bhairab, because of some technical trouble they were having with a Boeing 747. Did it work? Who knows, but something tells me they let trained engineers look at the plane, too.

Nothing wrong with taking a risk based on what you believe in, but like Joey would say, you gotta know where to draw the line. Ethan didn't, for instance, when he, acting as a tool of *The Rule*, broke into the GameStore at the local mall and stole that Xbox 360 he gave to Landon. No mere math teacher, GameStore had way cooler security cameras, so the full-color hi-res images they captured were quickly and easily identified. Poor Landon had to give the Xbox back, but the police believed his story, probably because he sounded so damned disappointed.

The police, on a roll, also managed to match the GameStore images to the ones from Eldridge's driveway. When Ethan's lawyer dad saw how closely they matched his son's size, body type, and predilection for shiny white shoelaces, he stopped talking about suing and started making arrangements for a long vacation for Ethan at an out-of-state facility guaranteed to knock some sense into him.

In a way, Ethan did everyone a favor by kicking down the gym. Moore, back from suspension, discovered that the structure was flawed the same way it had been the first two times and that it probably would've collapsed on its own during the next heavy snow. This time they had insurance, though, and the gym was quickly rebuilt a third time, with a lot of inspectors watching. So far, it hasn't fallen down again. And *The Otus* won some sort of journalism award.

Maybe part of Ethan planned it all that way. Really, who knows?

As for what the hell the bamboo plane–building Vanuatu had to do with any of this, it took Mr. Eldridge to finally clear that up for me. We were chatting after trig his first week back when I mentioned the documentary. I was surprised to learn he'd seen it. A lot of *Mondo Cane* was what he called "arrogantly Eurocentric," meaning it defined weird as what a European would look down on because he didn't understand it. Really, the man should be teaching social studies if he weren't so good at math.

He also said the Vanuatu were interesting because they were imitating something true and important (airplanes) but didn't "get" it because they made it about their greed. Their bamboo planes didn't fly because the cargo cult wasn't interested in flying—they just wanted the cargo, the stuff.

Whammo! It hit me. Moore had been saying that *The Rule of Won* and the people who followed it were just like the Vanuatu, imitating the edge of something true and important, but missing the point entirely by making it about their own petty ideas about what they thought they should have.

There's a joke that I think makes the point nicely. It's got God in it, but it works even if you don't believe in God.

There's this guy who hears the news on the radio about a coming flood. Rather than panic, he reminds himself that all is well, God will provide. A while later, the flood's so bad he has to go up to the second floor of his house. Outside, he sees his neighbors in a boat.

They call out to him, "Come with us!"

"No thanks," he says. "God will provide."

A little later, the water's still rising and he's up on the roof. A police helicopter flies by to rescue him. "No thanks," he says. "God will provide."

So, he drowns. When he meets God in heaven, he says, "I don't understand. Why didn't you provide?" To which God replies, "What, are you kidding? I sent you a message, a boat, and a helicopter!"

Get it?

I heard Vicky and Grace tried to have one more Crave, to try to make the charges against Ethan go away, but only three people showed. A local band of Screech Neck dropouts had a video on YouTube that was getting, like, a million hits, and kids were much more interested in that than an Xbox 360 thief. I don't know if people lost faith in the book or just lost interest. Probably a combination of both.

Me? No big surprise, but it turns out I really do have major feelings for Erica. We're seeing each other now and I'm pretty happy about it, though whenever I see her writing, I get a little twinge. I try not to peek, but sometimes I do anyway, just to make sure. Twice a week, we get together to study algebra. She passed her first big exam last week.

Business for GP Joey, meanwhile, has been booming. Biodiesel, it turns out, is the wave of the future, so now he has a new rush of diesel engines to practice his skills on. Things are going so well, he's thinking of hiring Mom full-time to help out with the books. There's talk of an actual vacation.

And yes, this summer I plan to get a job, just to help out a little.

I've got only one question left. I asked Alden and Mr. Eldridge about it, but even they had no idea. They did think it was a good question, though.

If the Cravers are all just Vanuatu, who's flying the real airplane?

- The board's been quiet lately, but I'm not giving up! I imanifest for an hour every night that everyone's coming back big-time! Sure, there are bound to be a few stumbling blocks on the road to success, but everyone knows deep down the basic ideas we were practicing are good ones! Never give up and you never lose! And guess what? Jasper Trelawney has a new book coming out, *The Rule of Won for Teens*. I just know I'll find all the answers there. —Grace

EPILOGUE

Sunlight, slicing the Screech Neck gray, cut into Alyssa Skinson's room, making burning white rectangles on her drafting table. She still had her lamp on, though, just to make certain she could see exactly what she was working on.

Dad out shopping, she was alone, wearing her mother's old bathrobe over her newly washed pink and green leggings. She was hunched over, putting the final touches on a drawing of a new set of Prismacolor markers, the set her father laughed about when he saw how much they were. They were supposed to be the best in the world.

She'd been at it for hours, using pencil and crayon, marker, paint and pen, getting the lines, the lettering, even the light reflecting on the metal box just right. It was the first drawing she'd tried since the one of Caleb Dunne getting that video he was looking for. Ethan would be so angry if he knew about that.

But Ethan never understood. It was silly to believe the world was built just to give you whatever you wanted. More like you could ask, and it could still say no, and then you could say, "Well, how about this instead?" And it could say, "Well, maybe."

She hoped when he came back he wouldn't be so crazy, if he didn't die in that camp. She hoped he'd slip his feet in and out of his sneakers the old way, without bothering to untie the laces. Things could still be good again. Never perfect without Mom, but still good.

There. Finished. It was as close as she was going to get anyway.

The doorbell rang. Who could that be?

She scampered down the stairs, opened the door, and smiled at the white-haired delivery man as he handed her a box.

Her name wasn't on it, no name was, but she opened it just the same. She hated the Styrofoam popcorn, but at least it was the good kind, the green kind, the kind that dissolved in water and ran down the drain.

When she saw what was in it, her mouth curved into a perfect circle. Her heart beat faster and her body actually shook from the happy surprise. The markers! The full set! So much like the picture she'd drawn.

With these she could make every color in the rainbow. Even an aurora borealis.

And her pictures would never be garish. Not garish at all.

Acknowledgments

I really have no one to thank except the universe itself, since all I had to do was spend a lot of time picturing this book—one morning I woke up, and there it was!

Shoe-making elves could do no better.

But seriously, many thanks to publisher Emily Easton and editor Stacy Cantor for—aside from their hard work—the lunch conversation a year or so ago that solidified the character of Alyssa and gave me the idea for the *pro* and *epi* logues that I think add a lot to *The Rule*.

I'd be utterly remiss if I didn't also thank the long history of you-can-have-it-all books that have appeared over the last century, running the gambit from the *Science of Getting Rich* to Shirley MacLaine's *Out on a Limb* (it was in her work I first heard the odd notion that other people don't really exist) to the latest, and I'm sure not the last, *The Secret*.

As always, thanks to Sarah for her constant love and support, and my daughters, Maia and Margo, for never ceasing to surprise me with joy. You guys are swell.

Lastly, since before my work on the *X-Files* comic, on into my first self-published novel, *Making God,* and beyond, I've been lucky to be able to write about my fascination with the borderlands of what people believe and why; so, yes, many thanks to the universe, since it's really been pretty cool about the whole thing.